A Deadly Course

A Sugarbury Falls Mystery

by

Diane Weiner

For information, email **Cozy Cat Press**, cozycatpress@aol.com or visit our website at: www.cozycatpress.com

COZY CAT
P R E S S

ISBN: 978-1-939816-96-2

Printed in the United States of America

Cover design by Paula Ellenberger
www.paulaellenberger.com

1 2 3 4 5 6 7 8 9 10

Acknowledgements:

Many thanks to Eric Weiner and Mitch Garnick for
their medical/pharmacological guidance.

Dedication:

This book is dedicated to Patricia Rockwell for making
my dream of being an author come true.

Chapter 1

Emily Fox pulled her ponytail tighter. She had just cut her shoulder length auburn hair into a stylish bob, but now she struggled to pull it back for her run. Green velvet hills, a crystal clear lake, and a canopy of lush trees made her feel as though she was running through the Garden of Eden. When her in-laws had passed away, she and her husband Henry had inherited a Lincoln Log cabin on a lake aptly named Lake Pleasant, in Sugarbury Falls, Vermont.

It had been six months since she and Henry, both in their mid-fifties, had semi-retired, leaving their home in Upstate New York behind. Quitting her job at the newspaper to write full-time and teach a few classes at a small liberal arts college, Henry giving up his full-time radiology position at the hospital? No, she wasn't dreaming.

During her run, she mentally planned the agenda for the opening of tomorrow's summer writing camp. She taught journalism and creative writing at St. Edwards College and was thrilled when she was asked to lead a writing camp for adults. Six adults, mostly from out of state, had registered for the class. Emily planned to focus on fiction writing this session and ran through her day. First, she'd have an icebreaker activity so the participants would get a chance to get to know one another. Developing trust was essential in getting the participants to share their work and accept criticism from their peers. Then she'd have them brainstorm ideas. She wiped her sweaty face with the bottom of her sweaty singlet. Fruitless at best.

It's beastly hot for 8 a.m. I'm glad I came prepared. She stopped at the side of the road to gulp from her water bottle. As she tucked her bottle back into its holder, she glanced down the steep ravine which surrounded the path. *What's that down there? A dead animal?* She moved closer to the edge, then tentatively made her way down the rocky, root-laden hill. Near the bottom, her heart thumped and she let out a scream. *Oh my God. It can't be.* "Hey, are you okay?"

No answer. No sign of movement. She ran to where a biker lay tangled under his mountain bike, next to a solid tree. "I said, are you okay? Can you hear me?" It was a rhetorical question. Knowing she had to look past the horror of the situation, she checked his unnaturally twisted, bloody neck for a pulse and watched his chest for indications of breathing.

What do I do first? 911 or CPR? One of his legs was bent under him. It was most certainly broken. Still, no pulse. *I'll try CPR just in case I'm missing something.* When her arms tired from doing chest compressions and there was still no sign of breathing, she whipped her cellphone out of her waist belt and called 911.

"There's a biker down at the bottom of the ravine on Lake Pleasant Road. It's about halfway between The Outside Inn and the Reynolds' cabin. Hurry."

"Ma'am, help is on the way. Don't move him. Do you know CPR?"

"I've been doing CPR and nothing's happening. I'm afraid he's…I'm worried he's…"

"Police and ambulance will be there soon."

She paced around the body. He was wearing a helmet and the bike looked expensive. What caused him to go over the side of the road like that? He looked to be maybe in his early forties, in good shape, and wearing bike clothing that looked professional, yet not brand new. He wasn't new to the sport, and the roads were dry. It hadn't rained in days. She examined the ground looking for skid marks, but there weren't any. She considered the possibility of an animal crossing his path, but deer rarely came out once the early morning joggers and commuters emerged.

Sirens, finally. She yelled up the hill, hands cupped around her mouth. "He's down here!"

Two police officers, and two EMTs wielding a heavy duty backboard and a few portable instruments hustled down to the body.

"He's not breathing. I didn't find a pulse."

"We'll take it from here, ma'am."

She watched as they tried the defibrillator, gave him some sort of injection, then shook their heads and moved him onto the backboard. *He can't be. Please, God, don't let him be…dead.*

While the EMTs carried the man up the hill, the police questioned her. It was a small town, and she knew both officers.

"Tell us what happened."

"I was on my daily run. I stopped to drink water. Then I looked down and saw him. At first I thought it was some kind of dead animal. When I got closer, I asked if he was okay. He didn't say anything. He wasn't moving…"

"Mrs. Fox, do you have any idea who this man is? He wasn't carrying identification."

"I haven't lived here all that long, but I've never seen him before."

"Go on home. If we need more information I'll contact you. Do you need a ride?"

"I'd appreciate that."

When she got home, she collapsed on her over-stuffed sofa. Chester, her black cat, jumped up on her lap, startling her. She stroked his fur and began to calm down. Chester was a comfort, but she wished Henry hadn't gone to the hospital today. Although he'd retired before they moved, when confronted with the shortage of medical care in Sugarbury Falls, he'd accepted an offer to work part time for the local hospital. She got voicemail when she tried calling, no answer when she texted. She took a long shower and made herself a cup of tea. Afterwards, she called the police station to see if they'd made an identification. They hadn't as of yet.

Hours later, Henry came through the door. He ran over and hugged her. "Are you okay? I was tied up in the emergency room and didn't have my phone until later. You were the one who found the dead biker this morning?"

Not wanting to alarm him, her message had simply been to come home. "How did you hear...I didn't say...Never mind." In the short time they'd lived here, Emily knew how fast news and gossip flew in this small town.

"I heard he was already dead when you found him."

"He probably broke his neck during the fall."

"The injury wasn't severe enough to kill him. I talked to Pat." Pat was the medical examiner and had become Henry's best friend.

"How did he die, then?"

"Pat has ruled out injury as well as the most common natural causes. Couldn't get into details, but he thinks the guy may have been poisoned. He sent a bunch of samples to the toxicology lab in Burlington for testing. Thinks maybe foul play was involved."

"Foul play?"

"The guy was in great shape and his injuries weren't severe enough to kill him, so yes. He thinks the dead biker was murdered."

Chapter 2

Emily tossed and turned all night long in her king-sized, four-poster bed. She couldn't get the image of the mangled biker out of her mind. She pulled the quilt up to her neck. The suggestion that he'd been murdered was even more upsetting.

When she got a whiff of freshly brewed coffee, she padded down the ladder from their master bedroom loft, across the living room, and into the kitchen.

"Thanks, Henry. I'm going to need lots of coffee this morning. It's going to be hard to focus on teaching after yesterday."

"I'm sure it will." He fiddled with the Fit-Bit on his wrist.

"You know, I was trying to figure out how this man died. If it wasn't from his injuries, it doesn't mean it was murder. Maybe he got stung by an insect he was allergic to, or bitten by a snake. I've heard there are rattlesnakes in the woods."

Henry said, "The rattlesnakes around here are an endangered species, and the garter snakes you see aren't poisonous, so I don't think a snake bite is the cause."

"Look, they don't even know who the guy is yet. Pat likes to play Quincy, you've said it yourself. He wasn't shot or run over by a car. Why did he jump to the conclusion he was murdered? How long did he actually spend looking for a cause of death?"

"I guess you're right, but Pat is a cracker-jack medical examiner, one of the best in his field. His instincts are always spot on, and he found no logical reason for this man to be dead. All his organs looked normal. No aneurysm, no heart attack… The standard toxicology screen didn't show anything abnormal, so he sent the samples out to a more sophisticated lab."

"So everything looked perfectly normal and he didn't die from his injuries. The police will investigate and figure out who he is, but—I just had a thought. I hope he didn't have a family. Imagine hearing that kind of news?"

Henry kissed the top of her head. "I can't imagine. I've got to get to the hospital."

"Since when are you in such a hurry? You're hoping there's a puzzle to solve."

"You know me too well. I'm sorry about this poor fellow dying, but we owe it to him to figure out what happened, murder or not. And especially to his family, if he has one. Have a good first day at camp."

Emily sat at the butcher-block table and finished her coffee, then jumped into the shower. No run this morning. She combed out her newly chic auburn hair. Aiming for professional yet relaxed, she selected a pair of white linen pants and a breezy, short-sleeved blouse, chocolate brown, like her eyes. Chester was curled up on the quilt, but as usual, leapt off the moment Emily turned on the hair dryer. She ran her fingers through her hair. *I look a good five years younger. I should have done this sooner.*

When she arrived at her assigned classroom, two students were already there, waiting. Early birds. At least two of her six were eager to start. She introduced herself.

"I'm Emily Fox, the instructor."

"You need no introduction. I just finished reading your true crime book about the Ashley Young case.

Couldn't put it down. I'm Tessa Carlisle. So excited to meet you."

Tessa, dressed in a tailored pant suit, extended her hand. Emily guessed she was in her early sixties, with soft gray hair and designer framed eye glasses.

"Where are you from, Tessa? And what type of writing do you do?"

"I'm from Boston. I'm a retired pharmacist hoping to start a second career as a mystery writer."

"I should have known from your accent that you were from Boston. Welcome."

The other early bird, a slightly chunky man in a polo shirt with sandy-colored curls and a hint of a southern drawl said, "I'd like to start a new career too. I've been teaching elementary school for the past fifteen years. I love what I do, but the money stinks. I told myself I was coming so I could learn new ideas for teaching my students how to write fiction, but I have an ulterior motive. I want to be the next James Patterson." He chuckled. "My name's Logan. Logan Park."

"Where are you from Mr. Patterson? Oh, excuse me, Mr. Park." asked Emily, smiling.

"Grew up in the western part of North Carolina, then went to college in Chapel Hill. Afterwards, I relocated to Rochester, New York."

So far, so good. Both of these students were pleasant and seemed motivated. A dark-haired woman with olive skin and a New York accent walked through the door and introduced herself as Holly Jenson.

Emily's first thought was that this lady had to be a mom, most likely of a young child. She wore baggy jeans, and her hair was pulled into a no-nonsense pony tail. Emily thought she'd be stunningly pretty with a chic hairdo, clothes that fit her body, and a bit of makeup. The woman scanned the room with her dark eyes, as if looking for someone.

"I'm Holly Jenson. I just moved here with my son, Jimmy. He's three. My father has a place here. My husband is supposed to be coming too. He still lives and works in New York City and is meeting us for the camp." Her eyes shifted down and to the left when she spoke. Didn't that mean she was lying? Emily'd read that somewhere, maybe in one of Henry's private eye books that he left all over the house. Or was it looking right that was bad? She couldn't quite remember. And why weren't Holly and her husband living together?

Tessa and Logan made small talk with Holly, while Emily organized her notes. So far, this was a good mix. A retired pharmacist, a teacher, and a mom who'd just moved to the area.

Student number four came in. He was tall and slender. *Tall enough to be a basketball player*, thought Emily.

"I'm Wichita Johnson. Came up from the city. My partner and I are working on a new software bundle. It's called Story-WOW-ica@. If it makes the kind of splash my partner made when he developed Matha-WOW-ica@, we'll both be rich. Well, he's already rich. I came aboard after he struck gold with Matha-WOW-ica@." He smiled at Holly. "Holly, glad you made it. Where's Carter?"

Holly glared at him. "He was supposed to meet us here. Late as usual."

Emily said, "The two of you know each other?"

"Yes," said Wichita. "Holly's Carter's wife. The three of us all have a stake in the new product; that's why we came here. Wanted to make sure we were on track with this new writing program and figured we'd learn from an expert."

"I'm the computer consultant," said Holly. "Wichita *works* for my husband. He's not a partner."

"Not yet, but you wait and see," said Wichita.

It was fifteen minutes past the time the class was scheduled to begin. Emily decided to go ahead and start the icebreaker. The missing two would have to catch up. Emily was a stickler about time and her pet peeve was people who somehow never learned to read a clock. She handed out what looked like Bingo cards. The squares had things like 'lived in a foreign country,' 'own a dog,' and 'play a musical instrument.' The idea was to walk around and find others with a commonality, and they would initial that square.

"Everyone has a card, right?" Just as she was handing out markers, a woman about the same age as Tessa came in. She was slightly overweight, with straight, black hair.

"I'm so sorry I'm late. I took a wrong turn. I'm terrible with directions." She caught her breath and introduced herself. "I'm Maria Mendez. I write teen fiction. I'm a librarian from San Diego."

"San Diego?" said Logan. "That's a heck of a long way."

"I saw the advertisement for the camp on-line. When I saw it was being led by Emily Fox, well, I had to come. Mrs. Fox, I read your book about the Ashley Young case and was fascinated by it. You are quite the author."

"Thanks. Nice to meet you," said Emily. "Now that most of us are here…"

"Excuse us." Two men in suits walked into the classroom. Emily recognized them as local police. Detective Ron Wooster was in his thirties but with his baby face and athletic build, he appeared much younger. Detective Megan O'Leary was a beautiful red-head about the same age as her partner.

"I hate to interrupt, Mrs. Fox," said Detective Wooster, "but may I have a word with," he looked at his notes, "Mrs. Holly Jenson?"

"I'm Holly Jenson. What's this about?"

"Not here." Detective Wooster led her into the hall. "I'm afraid it's about your husband, Carter Jenson."

"Who did he piss off this time? Is it another law suit?"

"No, ma'am. He was found at the bottom of a ravine not far from here yesterday morning. His bike went over the side of the road. His injuries…"

"Whoa. My husband was in New York yesterday. He was supposed to fly in early this morning but hasn't shown up yet. He's supposed to be in class with me right now. You have the wrong person."

"Why don't you come with us to identify the body?"

Holly insisted the police had it wrong. Emily could hear her sobbing and came out into the hall.

"What's wrong? Holly, are you okay?"

"They…they think my husband is dead. They say he was in a bike accident yesterday. He wasn't supposed to arrive until today."

Emily's heart nearly stopped. A bike accident? Yesterday? What are the chances two bikers died yesterday? No, it had to be Holly's husband she'd discovered. Her legs felt like wet noodles.

Detective Wooster said, "Mrs. Fox, it's our understanding that you discovered the body."

Holly Jenson's jaw dropped. "You. You found my husband? He was already here?"

"I was running yesterday morning and I saw a man over the side of the ravine."

The other detective Megan O'Leary said, "Mrs. Fox tried her best to save him, Mrs. Jenson. She performed CPR and called 911."

"But…you say he's dead? I have to see for myself."

At that moment, Wichita Johnson stepped into the hallway. "Holly? Is something wrong? Why are the police here?" His eyes darted back and forth between the detectives.

"They say Carter is dead. He was involved in a bike accident."

"Bike accident? No way. Carter was an expert rider. Anyway, what was he doing riding when he was supposed to be packing to come here?"

Holly said, "They say he was already here. With his bike, no less. I don't understand."

"Mrs. Jenson, let's go identify the body and then go over to the station so we can begin piecing this together," said Detective Wooster.

"Identify the body? Then you aren't sure it's him."

"We matched his fingerprints to the military database and got our identification from there."

"He...he was in the army for a short time when we were first married."

Wichita put his arm around Holly's shoulder. "I'm going with you. It has to be a mistake. None of this makes sense."

Emily's mind raced. Neither the dead biker's wife nor his business partner knew he was already in town. What secret was he keeping? The first thing that popped into her mind was that he had a mistress nearby. She dismissed it, and decided that maybe the man just needed a few days to himself with such a stressful job and all. Then again, the medical examiner thinks something's off, she remembered. Pat has quite the creative bent, especially rare for a man in his position, however, he didn't find an obvious cause of death.

"Mrs. Fox, are you coming back in? You're not canceling our session, I hope," called out Tessa Carlisle.

Emily couldn't do that to them. They'd traveled a long way and paid for this experience. "No, I'm not leaving. Let's get to work."

Chapter 3

The morning flew by. The participants had all written a short summary of the story they planned to start writing during the summer. Tessa was planning a classic who-dunnit. Maria was planning a work in which a select group of highly intelligent teens overthrow the government and get the country back on track, and Logan envisioned a spy thriller. The participants were all staying at the Sugarbury Outside Inn, a bed and breakfast run by Emily's friend, Coralee Saunders.

"The Outside Inn has the best food around. I suggest going there for lunch," said Emily.

"If their lunch is anything like their breakfast, I'm in," said Logan. "I had the best blueberry pancakes I've ever eaten there this morning."

The inn was painted a sunny yellow with white trim and looked like it had popped out of the pages of a fairy tale. A porch, sporting wicker rockers, wooden Adirondack chairs, and a swing, wrapped around the building. A few guests sat on the porch, reading or doing crossword puzzles. Emily was happy to walk into the air conditioning.

Coralee, a doughy-skinned lady with sparkling eyes and a warm smile, greeted them. "Nice to see you all back for lunch." She counted the participants. "Did you lose a few along the way?"

"It's a long story," said Emily. "Turns out the dead biker I found yesterday morning was registered for my workshop. So are his wife and his business associate.

The police came by and needed someone to identify the body and those two went with them. Like I said, it's a long story."

Emily realized something she hadn't thought about. "He must have been staying here like the rest of the participants. I'm sure you met him, Coralee."

"No, I didn't. A Carter Jenson had a reservation but never checked in."

"That's strange. He was out riding early in the morning. I assumed he'd have been here the night before."

"Wasn't here, I'm sure of that. Follow me, everyone. Do you prefer to sit inside or on the patio?"

"I'm not used to this heat," said Maria. "If it's agreeable, I'd prefer inside."

Emily was all in favor of being comfortable too. Coralee handed them lunch menus and described the mouth-watering specials—grilled vegetable and Brie Panini, clam chowder, and a strawberry-walnut salad topped with goat cheese.

Coralee's handyman, Franklin Matherson, a middle-aged gentleman with weathered hands and a full head of hair, ran up to the table. Tessa whispered, "What a hunk. He looks just like Tom Selleck."

"I spotted him first," said Maria.

"Coralee," the man said, "I have an emergency. I need to get down to the police station."

"What's wrong Franklin?"

"It's my son-in-law. He died in a biking accident yesterday. My daughter is at the station. I didn't even know he was already in town. Why didn't he let us know he was here early? Holly needs me."

Coralee said, "Go on. Take whatever time you need."

Tessa said, "Poor man."

"Looks like he'll need a bit of consoling," said Maria.

Emily's head felt like a volcano about to erupt. How much more could she handle? Carter Jenson was Franklin Matherson's son in law? Now it made sense. Holly had moved up here to be with her father.

"Coralee, did you know Franklin's daughter was moving in with him?"

"He mentioned it. His grandson's here too. Franklin saw the flier for your summer camp and told Holly about it. Guess that explains how her husband knew about it."

"I don't know about the rest of you, but my stomach is growling," said Logan. "I'll take the clam chowder and the panini!"

"I'll get right on it," said Coralee.

Chapter 4

Henry hadn't gotten a minute to breathe all morning. He was helping out in the emergency room and in the past three hours had pushed a dislocated shoulder back into its socket, bandaged a sprained ankle, treated a bad case of poison ivy, prescribed cough syrup for a toddler with a hacking cough, and refilled an inhaler for an asthmatic. Practicing medicine here was much more varied than practicing radiology back in New York had been.

Pat Hester, the medical examiner, popped into his office. "Hey, buddy, want to grab some lunch?"

"Sounds good. Cafeteria?"

"Yeah." He started walking toward the elevator.

"No," said Henry, "let's take the stairs. I want to get in a few more steps." He checked his wrist. Competitive as he was, no one in his Fit-Bit group was going to outwalk him.

"I have to get back to work on the biker this afternoon. I finished the autopsy and I'm still puzzled over cause of death," said Pat. "I'm going to send a few other samples out for a more comprehensive screening. Could take a few days to get the results back, though if the detectives call the lab, they'll be more likely to rush it."

"Did you look for bite marks? Needle marks? Heat exhaustion?"

"Come on, Henry. Of course I did. The man's wife identified him this morning. Guy's name is Carter Jenson. He owned a software business in New York. He was up here for Emily's writing camp. So was his wife and business associate."

They took the steps down and walked into the noisy, brightly lit cafeteria. Pat handed Henry a tray and they proceeded through the line.

"A software exec coming to a writing camp?"

"His wife said something about him working on an educational writing program. How's Emily doing?"

"She's still a bit rattled. I called her a little while ago. She was taken aback when she realized the dead biker she found yesterday was supposed to have been in her class."

They grabbed a table near the exit. Henry took out his travel-sized hand sanitizer and bathed his hands in it.

"Emily says Carter Jenson hadn't shown up at Coralee's place either. He had a reservation for two days ago. If he wasn't staying at the Outside Inn, then where did he stay?"

"There are only two other hotels nearby. There's a Holiday Inn and another privately owned bed and breakfast."

"But why make a reservation at one place, have your credit card charged for not showing up there, and show up at a different hotel? I don't know anyone who'd do that. Hotel rooms aren't cheap." Henry shoved the last bite of tuna sandwich into his mouth and swallowed the rest of his iced tea.

"Guy owned a successful company from what I hear. Maybe he has dollars to burn, who knows. I'm going to have to head back upstairs. You going home?"

"Yes, but I may make a stop or two first."

Henry checked his GPS for directions to the Holiday Inn. If Carter Jenson was staying somewhere other than Coralee's, he had to have been hiding something—

probably a mistress. The woman might still be around and if so could shed some light on the situation. If she'd already left, the police needed to track her down ASAP for questioning. The Holiday Inn was coming up on the left. He took the parking spot furthest from the door.

After marching up to the front desk, looking as confident as possible, he said, "I'm here to meet a friend, Carter Jenson. I forgot what room he's in. Would you mind checking?"

The clerk typed in the name. "There's no guest here by that name."

"Maybe he already checked out. Could you look?"

Henry knew this was most likely against policy, but the clerk was young and eager to help.

"Give me a minute. No, we never had a guest by that name. Sorry."

Henry thanked the clerk and set out for the next place, a bed and breakfast. When he pulled into the last space in the parking lot, he wondered how it did any business with Coralee's much spiffier place minutes away. The white building needed a good power washing and the hedges begged for a good trimming. He hoped the owner would be as amenable as the clerk at the Holiday Inn had been. Two women were talking on the front porch.

"Look here in the newspaper. They found a dead man over on Lake Pleasant Road the other day. He was from out of state. Some sort of bike accident."

"I'm just glad he wasn't staying at my place. What a horrible thing to have one of our guests die."

Henry said, "Excuse me. I couldn't help overhearing. I saw the story on the news. You said he wasn't a guest here?"

"Nope. All our rooms are full. Didn't have any no shows all month."

"All your rooms are full? Darn. I was hoping to make a reservation. Can you tell me what other places are around here? Hotels or bed and breakfasts—doesn't matter which."

"Well, there's Coralee's place down the road. It's called the Outside Inn. She's usually filled to capacity during the summer months. There's a Holiday Inn down the street."

"I already stopped there. No luck. Any others?"

"Not real close to here. The next closest is the Ramada, about ten miles away."

"I'll try that. Guess I have no other choice. You have a lovely place here. Maybe next time."

Ten miles isn't so far. Might as well explore all my options. He turned on the Sirius radio in his Jeep and plugged the hotel into his GPS. The roads were devoid of traffic at this hour, and he hadn't even finished listening to the NPR podcast when he pulled in front of the three story Ramada Inn, hopeful he'd get the information he was looking for. Losing patience, he parked right in front of the entrance. The employee behind the desk was middle aged, with thick glasses, a neatly pressed uniform jacket, and a bow tie. Henry crossed his fingers.

"Excuse me. I have a friend who's staying here. I'm supposed to meet him but I forgot his room number. Can you pull it up for me?"

"I'm sorry, but I'm not permitted to do that. It's a privacy issue. If he's your friend, why don't you call his cellphone?"

Why don't I call his cellphone? Duh, I never thought of that.

Henry glanced at the activity board beside the desk and tried an alternate approach. "Hey, the map on your board shows there's a bike trail that starts behind the hotel. I'm an avid biker." *If spinning classes count.* He surprised himself at how easily that little fib came out of his mouth.

"Yep. Nice long one. Goes all the way into town and around Lake Pleasant."

"I'll bet lots of your guests take advantage of that."

"A fair amount do. We even have bikes for rent."

"I'll keep that in mind. I'm going to try my friend's cell. Thanks anyway."

Henry got back into his Jeep. On his way home, he called the Ramada Inn, hoping the front desk person wouldn't recognize his voice, which he'd attempted to disguise, using advice he'd read in a private investigator's manual.

"Hello. My wife and I are coming into town this weekend and I'd like to make a reservation. My name is Carter Jenson. *J E N S O N*. Yes, Friday night, two people. One night. Okay, Thanks."

I'm sure Emily won't mind a little get away. Especially when she finds out why.

Chapter 5

When Henry got home, Emily was still at the workshop. He pulled out his laptop, chased Chester off the keyboard, and googled Carter Jenson.

Born in Bergan County, New Jersey. Worked for a struggling software company. Developed a revolutionary software program for teaching math, which made him rich. He bought his own company in New York and was listed in Business Weekly*'s top ten CEO's in 2015.* He was so engrossed in his research, that he didn't hear Emily come in.

"Hi, hon." She gave him a kiss.

"You startled me. I'm digging up lots of background on your dead biker."

"He's not *my* dead biker. I can't get the image of his mangled body out of my head."

"I think you'll rest easier when we know what happened. I had lunch with Pat. He said no snake or insect bites. Then I did some legwork. I went around to other hotels in the area, since you told me Carter Jenson never made it to Coralee's."

"Did you find out where he stayed?"

"I ruled out the two places in town. Then I rode out to the Ramada Inn."

"Isn't that a little out of the way?"

"Yeah, but get this. They have a great biking path. It's even mentioned on their website. I have a feeling Carter stayed there."

"Let me guess. They wouldn't confirm it, right?"

"No. They played by the rules, but I know how we can find out. Want to take a romantic overnight to the Ramada on Friday?" He wrapped his arms around her from behind and kissed her neck.

"Ooh. How could I resist? What's your plan, handsome fella?" She looked into his sparkly blue eyes.

"Well…" He heard a knock and looked from Emily to the door and back again. He sighed. "To be continued. I'll get it."

Henry led Detective Wooster into the living room. "What can we do for you?"

"I wanted to ask Mrs. Fox a few more questions."

"Please, have a seat. Ask away."

Detective Wooster sat in the rocking chair in front of the fireplace. "I was wondering if you noticed anything else about the morning you found the biker. Had you passed him on the road earlier? Did you notice maybe a car either speeding or going slow—maybe looking for someone?"

"No. I didn't see any other bikers, runners, or walkers for that matter. The traffic was like usual. Nothing remarkable."

"Did you hear anything? Maybe an unusual noise? An odor?"

Emily thought for a moment. "No, I wish I could be more help."

"It's okay. It's an open investigation and we're making sure we don't miss anything. Was Mrs. Jenson at the workshop today?"

"Yes. She said she wanted to keep her mind busy. She was anxious to plan a funeral and have closure."

"I know. I told her we couldn't release the body yet."

Henry stood up. "Why's that? Why can't you release it?" Henry knew very well that they were investigating this as a potential murder, but played dumb, hoping to get some tidbit of information from the detective.

"Let's just say it's an open investigation. Thanks for your time. If you remember anything further..."

"I'll call you right away." Emily saw him out. She was disappointed in herself. There must have been something she missed which could have helped the police.

Henry plopped down on the couch. "Hungry?"

"Yes, but I don't feel like cooking."

At the same time, they said, "Coralee's."

Emily filled Chester's bowl, then washed her face and changed into a pair of capris. Henry, wearing plaid shorts and a red polo shirt, grabbed the keys. The sun was lower in the sky, but there was still a good hour of daylight left. When they got to the inn, three of her students—Tessa, Maria, and Logan—were seated at a table, pouring over the menus.

"Henry, these are some of my students. Tessa is a retired pharmacist. Maria came all the way from San Diego, and Logan is an elementary school teacher living in Rochester, New York. He's going to be the next James Patterson."

Logan laughed. "Don't I wish. Your wife is a fabulous teacher. I've learned so much already."

"Yeah, she's pretty amazing." Henry put his arm around Emily, and she ruffled his wavy blond hair.

"Why don't you join us?" asked Tessa.

Emily looked at Henry, who said, "Sure." They both sat down and perused the menus, as if they hadn't practically memorized them with as often as they ate there. Henry poured hand sanitizer into his palms and rubbed them together.

After ordering, Maria said, "Did you hear anything more about Holly's husband? I'm surprised she showed up at the workshop today. Poor dear. And she has a little boy. Losing your husband is bad enough, but suddenly being a single parent on top of it?"

"At least she's living with her father. I'm sure he'll be a big help. Wouldn't mind living with that hottie myself," said Tessa.

"Remember, I saw him first," said Maria. Looking at Henry's confused expression, she said, "We're talking about Franklin, the handyman here."

"Coralee's Franklin?" asked Henry. "Nice guy. And he wasn't always a handyman you know. He's a retired chemist. Smart man."

"He sure does have chemistry," said Tessa.

"And he's charming to boot," said Maria. "Easy on the eyes, too."

Coralee brought the food to the table herself. "Are we talking about Franklin? You're not the first female guests to take a shining to him." She set plates of glazed chicken potpie and pasta primavera on the table. "I grew those vegetables myself. I've got a lovely garden in back."

Logan took a bite of his pasta. "Wow, this is fabulous. I better do a few extra miles on the bike or take an extra-long walk to make up for this. My doctor's already on my back about my weight."

When they'd finished dinner, Henry and Emily stopped at the desk to say goodnight to Coralee. Wichita Johnson, wearing jeans and a Harvard t-shirt, was gathering packages off the counter.

"Here two days and you're already getting mail?" said Emily.

Wichita jumped. "Work stuff. Follows you everywhere. Now that Carter is gone, I'll have to keep things flowing smoothly so the stockholders don't panic."

"Well, don't work too hard," said Emily. "How's Holly doing?"

"Holding up better than most would under these circumstances. Little Jimmy's keeping her going. I'm sure money won't be a problem. She's going to inherit a small fortune, plus the company life insurance. Double being as how Carter's death was accidental. I can't believe he just tumbled off the ravine like he did."

"The police are still investigating. I'm sure they'll piece it together. See you in the morning."

Emily hoped she was right. *Double the life insurance? Inheriting the company? Holly was already in Sugarbury Falls with her Dad before Carter died. A possible mistress, lying about being in town...If Carter was murdered, Holly had a good solid motive for killing him.*

Chapter 6

Emily sat straight up in bed. *The water bottle. I saw a water bottle on the ground near Carter's body. I'll have to call the police in the morning. Double life insurance for accidental death? Wichita now ran the company. What if either Holly or Wichita poisoned Carter's water?*

Henry rolled over to face Emily. "Are you okay? It's the middle of the night."

"I just remembered seeing a water bottle near Carter's body. I wonder if the police collected it."

"It's not unusual that he'd have had a water bottle with him. For that matter, it may not have even been his. You're think someone tampered with it? No one knew he was already in town."

"As far as we know, no one knew."

"We're going to the Ramada Inn tonight. If he was staying there, I'm thinking he wasn't alone. I'll bet at least one other person knew he was in town. Now, let's get some sleep. I have to be at the hospital early and you have to teach."

Emily never did get back to sleep. At 5:30, Chester jumped on the bed, nudging her with his nose, rubbing against her, and walking on her back. It was his morning ritual but he was a little ahead of schedule today. Henry was already in the shower.

It's a little too early to call Detective Wooster. She sat at her desk and made a list of suspects and their motives. *Holly may have found out her husband was cheating on her. She also stood to inherit lots of money and a lucrative company upon Carter's death. Even more so if he died accidentally.* She made a new column. *Wichita is running the company now that Carter is dead. Now he's in the driver's seat.* She crossed out his name deciding his motive was too weak.

Henry, toweling off his hair, stepped out of the bathroom. "What'cha got there?" He peeked over her shoulder.

"A list of possible suspects, or should I say, suspect. I can't come up with much."

"Hmm, you don't really know Holly. Is it fair to assume she has the stomach for murder?"

"It's always the spouse, isn't it?" She laughed. Henry threw a pillow at her. She got up and pulled on a pair of running shorts and a top. "I'm going for a run before class. Looking forward to our overnight." She gave him a kiss and headed outside.

Since finding Carter, Emily had avoided the part of her route that took her past the accident site. Today she felt brave enough to resume her normal routine. Along the way, she scanned the sides of the road. *What is it I'm looking for? Surely the police have been through this area twenty times by now.* Up ahead, she saw a man in a neon t-shirt, baseball cap, and sunglasses, walking toward her.

"Franklin. Out for some exercise?" She'd seen him walking in the mornings on several other occasions.

"It's good for my heart. Maybe one day the doctor will let me get off my pills if I keep it up. Besides, Jimmy's already up and chattering a mile a minute while Holly's trying to get him dressed for tiny-tots camp. I need a bit of quiet time."

Emily turned around and walked beside Franklin. ""How's Holly doing?"

"Under the circumstances, not too bad. She's feeling guilty."

Alarms went off in Emily's head. *Guilty? Was I right to suspect her?* "Why should she feel guilty? It's not like she could have prevented his death."

"She and Carter had been having problems for a while. She took Jimmy and moved out here with me, kind of a trial separation. Wanted to clear her head and decide whether or not she wanted to stay married."

"Problems?"

"Yeah, same old story. He was taking off on mysterious 'business trips,' making calls on his cellphone and hanging up when she came in the room. You can imagine what it looked like."

"Poor thing."

"She's better off without him. Caused my baby so much heartache. Last straw was him threatening to get sole custody of Jimmy if she left him."

"He wouldn't have gotten custody if he was cheating on her. Besides, the judge generally sides with the mother."

"Carter was rich and well connected. Holly knew he had half the judges in town in his back pocket. And then there was the pre-nup. If they'd gotten divorced, Holly wouldn't have gotten one red cent. And to top it off, she works at the company and would've been out of a job. He'd already been reminding her of that for years. I wanted to kill the bastard myself."

"Interesting. I hope it all works out for her here in Vermont. She's going to stay here, right?"

"She may have to run down to the city on occasion, but mostly she telecommutes. She can do her software magic from wherever. Wichita's gonna be overseeing the site and he'll let her know if he needs her. This is my stop. Nice chatting with you, Emily." He disappeared down a driveway.

Emily resumed running and headed home. She still had to take a shower, eat breakfast, and call Detective

Wooster about the water bottle before going to St. Edwards. By the time she got home, Henry was gone for the day. She took out the detective's card and called the station.

"This is Detective Wooster, How can I help you?"

"Detective, it's Emily Fox. I remembered something. There was a water bottle at the crime scene. It was just a few feet from Carter's body."

"Yes, we collected it into evidence."

"Were there any traces of poison?"

"Mrs. Fox, even if there were, I couldn't discuss that with you. Thanks for calling and have a great day."

She hated being dismissed like that. Pat Hester had told Henry he suspected foul play after completing the autopsy. Carter Jenson didn't die from his injuries, a bite, or heat exhaustion. Pat had told Henry that much. Poison made the most sense. She wondered if the lab in Burlington had finished analyzing the samples and gotten back to the police yet. She jumped into the shower and made it to St. Edwards just in time to start the workshop.

"My fingers are itching to write this morning," said Tessa. She was dressed in designer jeans and a short sleeved angora sweater. Emily smelled White Rain hairspray as she walked past her.

Everyone except Wichita was sitting at a desk, notebooks open. Wichita had been late nearly every day since the workshop had started. Emily remembered Holly making a comment about him being 'late as usual' the very first day.

"Today," said Emily, "let's go around and hear what each of you wrote as your elevator pitch. Remember, yesterday we talked about having a clear, two sentence summary of your book in mind before you start writing."

"I did my homework," said Tessa. "Can I go first?"

"You bet." Emily was tickled by Tessa's enthusiasm.

"While on a road trip to the Grand Canyon, a wife slowly poisons her husband with arsenic because she found out he's been having a twelve-year affair with her sister."

"Great. Arsenic is a tried and true poison and being on a long road trip, she could easily slip it to him. Who's next?"

Logan, the elementary school teacher from Rochester, raised his hand. "Me, me, me."

"You're very good at playing the role of student," said Emily. "Let's hear it, Mr. Patterson."

"When a man discovers his employer has stolen his idea for a new product, he spies on him, finding that his boss has many enemies. Soon the boss is dead and everyone in the office is a suspect."

"Sounds like the makings of a thriller if you add some action and a sprinkle of gory description. Good job."

Wichita, hair uncombed and wearing the same shirt he had on the day before, came in, apologizing for his tardiness. "I was up half the night on a business call but I've had my coffee and I'm ready to go."

Holly shook her head. "Try to have a little respect for other people's time, Wichita."

"Hey, I paid for this workshop the same as the rest of you. If I'm late, it's on my dime, but thanks for the advice, Holly."

The rest of the day, the group sketched out their major plot points. Emily gave them examples from best sellers and had them work together to analyze the excerpts. Because she was anxious to get home and pack for her weekend getaway, the time dragged like a trailer being pulled through mud, but eventually it was time to go home and get ready.

"Henry, are you all packed?"

"Just about. What happened when you called Detective Wooster about the water bottle?"

"Nothing. He said they'd already collected it into evidence and 'Have a nice day.' Hey, I already packed last night so I'm ready when you are."

They got into Emily's new Audi rather than the Jeep. She breathed in the new car smell and reclined the passenger seat. If the hotel happened to have valet parking…well, let's say she felt a sense of elegance pulling up in it. It didn't take long to reach the hotel. Behind on his daily steps goal, Henry found a spot far from the entrance. He peeked into the lobby, relieved to see a different front desk clerk than the one he'd spoken to the other day.

"We have a reservation. I prepaid."

"Name, sir."

"Carter Jenson." He gave Emily a little nudge to keep her from reacting.

"Here you go, sir. Enjoy your stay."

When they were out of earshot, Emily said, "What was that about?"

"You'll see. By the time we leave tomorrow, we'll know if Carter was with someone."

Chapter 7

Before dinner, Henry called the front desk. "Hello, this is Carter Jenson in Room 104. I wonder if you could do me a favor. I misplaced my bill for my last visit and I can't get reimbursed by my company without them. Could you pull up a duplicate copy?" Emily mouthed, 'What on earth are you doing?' Henry mouthed back, 'You'll see.'

"Let me see…yes," said the clerk, "I have two other stays this year to date. Do you want all of them?"

"That would be lovely. This place is always so accommodating."

Emily said, "I have to admit that was a clever move. Now we'll know if he was here with a girlfriend."

"We'll see if he ordered room service for two. Speaking of room service, what do you want to do about dinner?" Henry's phone vibrated. "It's Pat."

"Hey, Pat. We just got to the Ramada. What's up?"

"The results came back from the Burlington lab. The water bottle was clean, no traces of contaminants. No signs of poisoning. I personally reexamined the heart and blood vessels and again everything looked totally normal. There weren't any red flags in his medical history, either. Did they find a prescription or over the counter drugs with his things?"

Henry couldn't believe he hadn't thought of it sooner. Where were Carter's belongings? He was supposed to check into the Outside Inn the night before the workshop started but never showed up. He was riding his bike the morning before he had the reservation at Coralee's. Did he check out of the Ramada before his bike ride?

"Pat, I don't know where his things are. What do they do with a guest's things if they leave them behind?"

"See if they have some sort of lost and found there. I'm sure they must have tried calling him, but we know that wouldn't have worked."

"Okay, thanks, Buddy. I appreciate you keeping me in the loop."

Henry told Emily what Pat had said and suggested asking about the lost and found. They followed the desk clerk's directions and took the elevator to the basement level. The first door they passed had a sign next to it that read *Lost and Found*.

A young woman reading a romance novel sat at the desk. "Can I help you folks?"

"Yes. My name is Carter Jenson and during my last visit I left behind a few clothing items."

She looked over her shoulder. "Help yourself. The boxes are arranged according to date."

Henry and Emily rummaged through the correctly dated box, but found nothing that even looked like it belonged to a man. There was a woman's bathrobe and a pair of heels, as well as a pink phone charger.

"His things aren't here," Henry said to Emily. "My other guess is his car." Henry asked the woman at the desk about the car.

"If a guest has checked out and leaves his car behind, it would be towed away. Not that I remember that ever happening. I mean, who's gonna forget to take their car?"

"Where would they tow it?"

"A few miles down the road to a lot the town owns. I think they're open till nine."

"Thank you. We appreciate your help."

"Now what? asked Emily. "We have no idea what kind of car he drove and certainly can't march down to the lot with no proof of ownership and hope to get it even if we knew what we were looking for and even if it's there."

"Let's strategize over dinner. The hotel restaurant looks reasonable."

"Sure. Let's go up and change."

As they passed the front desk, Henry heard the clerk say, "Mr. Jenson." At first he kept walking, then realizing the clerk meant him, he responded, "Yes, do you need me?"

"I just wanted to give you that duplicate bill you asked for. I was going to call up to your room to tell you it was ready, then I saw you go by. Saves you another trip down."

"Thank you. That was quick." He took the bill and resisted going over them in front of the clerk. When they got back to the room, he devoured them line by line.

"What do you see?" said Emily. She tried to read over his shoulder but it was too difficult to see the small print.

Henry took a minute. "There are room service charges but it looks like he was alone. One order of scrambled eggs and bacon with an orange juice, an order of French toast the next morning, a club sandwich for lunch one day…He was here a whole week before you found him, Emily."

"How about the other stays?"

"Same thing. And both times he got the room with the two double beds. If it were a romantic rendezvous, wouldn't he have chosen a room with a king bed? They even have suites here with Jacuzzis in them. Now if it were me having an affair and I had his kind of money,

I'd definitely have gone for the king bed and the Jacuzzi."

"If you were staying here with a mistress, believe me, they would have found you drowned in that Jacuzzi! By me. But the rest of what you said makes sense. He seems to have been staying here alone. Why? For the great biking path?"

"He was here for a whole week this time, and also a whole week back a few months ago. His girlfriend could be local."

"Then they would have stayed at her place, don't you think? How about if I call Holly and find out what kind of car he drove?"

"No, that will seem weird. Let's eat dinner and tomorrow try the bike path, see if it gives us any clues. I'll wash my hands and be ready in a minute."

The food couldn't hold a candle to what they were used to at Coralee's, but it gave them a chance to go over the case once again. Emily vowed to talk to Holly first thing Monday morning to find out about the car and to ask if Carter had suffered from any health conditions.

"We don't have a Jacuzzi in the room, but I can see the pool from the window and it's deserted. What do you say, Em?"

"A moonlight swim with my boo? I'm in."

Early the next morning, they ordered room service for breakfast, then rented bikes in back of the hotel. The bike path was clearly marked and in total covered over twenty miles.

"Okay, let's go slowly and see if we find anything that can help us," said Emily.

As they rode, they each looked back and forth on either side of the trail, stopping at each of the regularly spaced rest areas, which included water fountains and bathrooms.

"I can hardly stand the smell. Look how full this garbage can is? I'll bet it hasn't been emptied since before Carter's murder."

"Emily, I'm done digging through garbage. We'd have no idea if any particular food wrapper or empty bottle belonged to Carter, anyway."

"I guess you're right. This is turning out to be a waste of time."

"We're getting in some exercise at least." He looked at his Fit-Bit. "Come on, let's finish what we started and check out the next one."

They rode until they hit the next rest area. Henry hopped off his bike and went into the men's room, which like the others along the trail, had a dirt floor and rusty sink. In spite of the grime-covered, tiny window up top, he could barely see. He'd been in Porta-Potties that smelled better. After his eyes adjusted to the dimness, he noticed something next to the toilet, under a pile of paper towels. It was a black waist pouch, kind of like an athletic version of a fanny pack.

I can see how this was overlooked. Someone trying to use the toilet may have unstrapped it from his waist, then forgotten to put it back on before leaving the bathroom. He ran outside to show Emily.

"Open it. Let's see what's in there." She watched him unzip it.

"There are a couple of Band-Aids, hand sanitizer, a few chocolate-flavored energy gel packs for long distance runs, and a room card."

"Do you think it was Carter's?"

"Em, I'd say that's a long shot, except for the fact that anyone else who lost it would have had a chance to come back for it. This is close to where you found Carter. He may not have realized he left it, or realized it and didn't have a chance to retrieve it."

"Let's get it to the police. Even though you touched it, there will still be prints from the owner. I hope Detective Wooster appreciates this."

Chapter 8

When they got back into town, they made a stop at the police station and spoke to Detective Wooster.

"We found this fanny pack in the men's bathroom along the bike path we believe Carter took. He was staying about ten miles outside of town at The Ramada Inn and they have this great bike trail…"

"Mrs. Fox, we know all about it. We've already been out to the Ramada Inn and we collected Mr. Jenson's belongings. We also have his car."

"You do? Did you find any prescription drugs?"

"Mrs. Fox, like I said before, I can't discuss this with you."

"Can you at least run prints and see if this fanny pack belonged to Carter Jenson?"

"Of course we will. Thanks for bringing it in."

Henry put his arm around her. "Let's go, Em. We did our part."

Back home, Henry and Emily unpacked, then foraged through the kitchen for dinner ideas.

"We have chicken in the fridge that needs to be used. I'll coat it in Panko crumbs and bake it. I'll throw a few potatoes in the oven, and you can make a salad. How's that sound?"

"It sounds like a plan. I'm going to check the mail first."

Emily got dinner started. *First thing Monday morning, I'm going to ask Holly if Carter had a heart condition. I'd like to tell her Carter was up here alone, but she hasn't confided in me that they were having*

*problems. That fanny pack has to belong to Carter. I
sure hope the police think to ask Holly to identify it. I'm
not sure it will be of any value now that Pat said there
weren't signs of poisoning.* She heard the door open.

"Hey, Em. There's an official-looking letter here
addressed to you. Looks like it's from a lawyer's
office."

She wiped her hands on the dish towel and took the
letter. "It's from Chicago. Who do I know in Chicago?"
She tore it open and read it silently. "Oh no." She read
further. "No way, it can't be."

"What can't be?" Henry tried to read over her
shoulder.

"I can't, we can't possibly do this." Her mouth
tightened.

"Do what?"

She put the letter down on the counter. "Do you
remember my college roommate, Fiona?"

"Of course. She was in our wedding. Does the letter
have something to do with Fiona?"

"Let's sit down. Fiona passed away suddenly. Some
sort of blood infection. I can't believe she's dead!" She
shook her head. "Anyhow, she had a daughter—
Madelyn. Fiona wasn't the marrying type, but when she
reached her upper thirties, she felt her biological clock
chiming and I mean loudly. She decided to become a
single mom."

"I remember when you got the birth announcement.
You've barely been in touch since."

"We'd sort of kept up on Facebook. I can't believe
she's gone."

"I'm sorry. I know you were once really close
friends."

"Here's the thing. Fiona had no family here. I think
there was an uncle back in Scotland, but her parents

died many years ago. Madelyn is the product of an anonymous donor, so there isn't a father in the picture."

"Cut to the chase. What are you saying?"

"She named me as Madelyn's guardian in the event of her death. The lawyer wants to arrange for us to pick her up and sign the legal work."

"You're kidding, right? She did that without even asking if you'd be willing?"

"Well, back in college it once came up. We both agreed we'd take care of each other's children if they became orphans. It was after a night of heavy drinking. I didn't take it seriously. Neither of us was even married yet."

"Apparently Fiona took it very seriously. We can't raise a child. This is crazy. You didn't ever want children after what happened with your sister. How old is this kid anyway?"

"She's fourteen. About to start high school. And the same age my sister was when...you know."

"You're not considering this, are you?"

"I don't know. I'm still in shock. If we don't take her, what will happen to her?"

"She'll go into the foster care system."

"No one is going to adopt a fourteen year old. She'll be shuffled around from family to family, or worse yet live in some sort of institution, and on top of it, she must be devastated over losing her mother."

"I don't know, Em. It's a lot to digest." He sniffed and looked around the room. "Hey, is something burning?"

"Oh, no. My chicken." She grabbed the pot holders and pulled out a sheet of charred chicken cutlets. "I can't think straight, Coralee's?"

"Coralee's."

Chapter 9

Emily stared at the ceiling all night long. How could she possibly raise a teenager, and why would she be crazy enough to try? She and Henry had a beautiful life together with the freedom to spend their time as they wished, freedom to enjoy financial comfort, and freedom to live a peaceful and virtually stress-free existence.

Henry rolled over in bed. "Are you okay?"

"A lot on my mind as you can imagine. Go back to sleep. We'll talk in the morning."

She had seen friends live through the teenage years. In the best cases, it meant butting heads, shelling out money, and coping with raging hormones. In the worst cases it meant dealing with drugs, alcohol, bullying, and even jail. Look at what poor Coralee went through with her son Noah. Imagine having your kid arrested?

Henry rolled back over. "I can't sleep now either. I know what you're thinking. If we don't take in Madelyn, then her life is ruined. She'll flit from school to school, be exposed to all sorts of atrocities, and spend her life working behind the counter of a donut shop because she never had the money to go to college…"

"I hadn't gotten that far. Poor Fiona. If we don't take her daughter, she'll never be able to rest in peace. She trusted me to take care of her child. That's heavy duty."

"Yeah, but at the time she was young and not even yet a parent. She probably didn't remember even saying it."

"It was in her will. According to the letter, the last draft was revised only a year ago. I'm still the one she trusted."

"Do you want to do this? I mean, we have the financial resources. This would be an excellent place to grow up." He hesitated. "What am I, crazy? I know nothing about being a father. I'd have to teach her how to drive, fight off the subpar boyfriends..."

"We can't make a decision this second. I have to get back to them by next week. Let's sit with the idea, and meanwhile, try to get some sleep." She clutched her Chill-ow and turned on her side.

"Goodnight." Henry closed his eyes.

Emily tried a relaxation techniques she'd read about. *Toes, relax. Calves, relax. All my worries are floating away from my body. Thighs, relax, stomach relax.* It wasn't working.

"Henry? Are you asleep?"

Henry groaned. "Not anymore."

"Do you think Chester would be jealous? He's been the only child for so long..."

"We'll ask him in the morning."

Somehow, they both managed to get in a few hours of sleep. Emily woke up first, and pulled on her running clothes. She did her best thinking when running. It was hot out but not as sticky as it would invariably become later in the day. At the end of her driveway, she ran into their neighbor, Kurt Olav with his chocolate Labrador, Prancer.

"Hi, Kurt. I see you shaved your beard down to a handsome stubble. That's in, you know. All the hot, young actors have a little stubble going." *Now if he'd just lose the lumberjack shirt...*

" It's cooler this way. I'll never like summer," said Kurt. "Give me my cold Minnesota winters any day. How was your overnight trip?"

Was that just yesterday? "Fine. We got in a nice long bike ride."

"Thought you might stay away from bikes for a while. Any news on the dead guy?"

"They still aren't sure how he died. It wasn't from the fall. Did you know he was Franklin's son-in-law?"

"Naw, you're kidding. Franklin hated his son-in-law. Was always picking up the pieces when his daughter came running to him after a fight. She'd moved in with him, you know. She and her son."

"The guy evidently had secrets. He was supposed to come up from New York the day before my workshop started. I told you how he and his wife were registered to be in my class. Poor Holly had no idea he'd been in town for a whole week before that."

"She had to have known."

"What makes you say that?"

"I ran into Holly at the general store last week. She was arguing with a guy who had to have been her husband. She was yelling at him about sneaking around with his girlfriend. He said just because *she* was a lying cheater it didn't mean he was one too."

"What else did you hear?"

"The guy said she'd better get her act together or she could kiss her son goodbye. She slapped him right there in the store. Then the owner kicked them both out."

"Wow, interesting." Filing away that information for further exploration, Emily changed the subject. "Kurt, how are things going with your daughter? She came to visit a few weeks ago, right?"

"I told you I don't like talking about Chloe." He grunted. "But things are on the right track. I'll say that much. You never stop worrying about them, even when they're all grown up."

"I'll bet it was hard, being a parent."

"Lots of work, but I wouldn't trade it for the world, even in spite of my problems with Chloe. Chloe was the happiest little girl ever. Always a smile on her face. I used to take her fishing back in Minnesota. We had a little garden in back of our house. She loved digging around in the dirt. Wouldn't dream of using worms for bait. We used bread instead. Little bits of stale bread. No wonder we never caught anything."

"Sounds like you have good memories."

"Like I said, I wouldn't have missed it, but I could have lived without all the drama, especially when she was a teenager. And then the whole divorce and custody fight."

Prancer barked and tugged at the leash.

"Big guy wants to keep moving. Dogs are the way to go. Keep you company and love you no matter what. And they never argue or ask for money."

Emily bent down and cupped Prancer's face, scratching him behind the ears. He reciprocated with a sloppy dog kiss. "Have a nice walk."

Emily walked for a few minutes to loosen up, then started her run. *So Holly knew Carter was already in town. Why did she lie? Carter called her a cheater? Was it Holly who was having the affair? Maybe Carter came up early to clear his head. Or to spy on Holly. She's looking guiltier by the minute.*

Chapter 10

Emily arrived at St. Edwards a few minutes early. Holly was the only student already there. *Just the person I wanted to see. Here goes.*

"Did you have a nice weekend, Holly?"

"I spent it looking online at caskets. Once Carter is buried, I can focus on healing and helping Jimmy move on. He keeps asking where Daddy is. I tell him he's in Heaven, then he asks when he's coming back. Makes my heart break."

Nice weekend? That was pretty insensitive of me. Holly just lost her husband. Even if they had problems in the relationship, I'm sure she's grieving. Unless, she's the one who killed him. She doesn't seem to be falling apart as much as I would be if I lost Henry.

"Death is an abstract concept for someone as young as Jimmy to understand. Holly, did Carter have a history of health problems?"

"Health problems? No way. The guy was healthy as a horse."

"So he didn't take any medications?"

"Only an occasional Advil. Why? Did you hear something more about his case?"

"I know as much as you do. They still haven't pinpointed a cause of death. I'm just thinking like a crime writer. Who would have wanted him dead, Holly?"

"I don't know. Me on occasion, but I didn't kill him."

"You know he was up here for a whole week before he died, right?"

Holly gasped. "What? No, of course I didn't. As far as I knew, he was in New York until the day before he was killed."

Holly is not a good actress. Emily heard chattering in the hallway. Tessa and Maria came in together, both sporting handmade clothing Emily had seen at the local craft fairs.

"Good Morning, Mrs. Fox. You know, I did a bunch of outlining over the weekend. I can't wait to get started," said Tessa.

"Morning, ladies," said Wichita. Surprisingly, he was on time.

Logan Park, wearing khaki shorts and an *I Love Vermont* t-shirt followed him in.

Emily said, "Today we're going to talk about motive. What motivates your characters to act in ways which further the plot? Tessa, your protagonist kills her husband to get even with him for cheating. What motivates the husband to act as he does?"

Tessa adjusted her glasses. "He feels guilty about the affair and tries to make it up to his wife by going on the trip."

"That's good. If you dig deeper, I'm sure you can correlate his actions to his motive. Holly, in your book, you have a single mother who goes down a sinister path. What's her motivation?"

"She wants to create the best life possible for her child."

"Even if creating the best path means, say, committing murder?"

Wichita's phone rang. "I forgot to turn off the ringer. I have to take this. Be right back." He stepped into the hallway.

"How rude, taking a call in the middle of our class," said Holly, shaking her head.

Emily, ignoring the comment but agreeing completely, told them to work independently and formulate a list of all the major characters in their works along with their motivations. While they were working, she wandered near the door, where she could hear Wichita's conversation.

"Yeah, doesn't change anything. In fact, it's even easier now without Carter snooping around over our shoulders. I got it. Yeah, I'll have it out in a couple of days."

What's easier? Was Wichita working against Carter? She moved away from the door just before Wichita came back inside.

"I apologize. It was somewhat of an emergency."

Emily explained the assignment and Wichita started writing. Before lunch, they shared their work with the group. Logan's main character was motivated by revenge. Maria's teen protagonist was motivated by fear.

"Fabulous job, all of you. Let's head over to the inn for lunch," said Emily. A crash of thunder shook the room. "Grab your umbrellas."

As they pulled up to the inn, Maria reapplied her bright red lipstick.

Tessa said, "Why are you putting on lipstick right before you eat? She fished in her purse for a mirror and started combing her hair

"Why are you combing your hair? It's raining. It's only going to get wet. Franklin only has eyes for me. We had a nice talk in the lobby yesterday afternoon. He asked me if I was going right back to San Diego after the workshop. I know he was hoping I'd stay longer."

Tessa said, "On Friday evening he asked me what plans I had for the weekend. He was going to ask me out, but he got shy."

"Let's go in and get some lunch. I'm starving," said Emily.

Walking to the inn, Logan whispered to Emily, "Those two are a hoot. I could write a book about them. Two women compete for the attention of a handsome widower and each plots to kill the other. Motivation: love. Or is it jealousy?" Emily laughed.

Coralee greeted them at the door. Wichita and Holly were driving together and hadn't yet arrived. "Follow me. I have a table for six waiting."

"Go ahead," said Emily. "I'm going to run to the restroom first." She smelled freshly baked bread, which made her stomach growl.

When she stepped out of the ladies room, Emily paused in the alcove. She heard Holly and Wichita talking in the lobby.

"Did you find what we needed?" said Holly. "Did you destroy the proof? We don't want anything coming out that will implicate us in Carter's murder."

"Of course I destroyed it. I'd have nothing to gain and plenty to lose. Now that Carter's dead, we're the only ones who know. Let's go before they wonder what's taking us so long."

Emily waited a few minutes, then joined the others at the table. Her head was spinning.

"We ordered you a Diet Coke," said Maria. "The specials are crab quiche and a bacon, Brie, and tomato sandwich on ciabatta bread. I'm having the quiche, myself."

"Thanks, Maria."

"Is something wrong?" asked Tessa. "Your body is here, but your mind isn't."

Emily had never been good at hiding her mood. She didn't let on that she'd just overheard a rather disturbing interchange, so she decided to go in another direction.

"I'm dealing with a bit of a personal dilemma. A friend of mine passed away suddenly. She wants Henry and me to raise her teenage daughter. We have to make a decision this week."

"Oh, my," said Tessa. "Are there other options for the girl if you decide not to take her in? Kids are tough. Especially teenagers."

"No good ones."

Logan said, "The poor girl. Over the years, I've had two students who lost parents. Completely destroyed them for a while. One was adopted by his aunt. Sweet, dedicated woman. Kept in close contact with me to make sure he was handling school okay. By the end of the year, he was coping surprisingly well."

"What about the other child?" said Holly.

"That unlucky boy had no one. I don't think his father was ever in the picture. Only option was for him to live with his maternal grandmother, but she refused to raise him. I understood. She had health issues and was barely able to get around."

"What happened to that boy?" asked Tessa.

"He went into the foster care system. He wound up going to three different schools before he got to middle school. Last I heard, he got into drugs. Police caught him selling weed to his classmates."

Coralee brought the food to the table herself. "Who was selling weed?"

"A student I once had who wound up in the foster care system," said Logan.

"Kids can get into all sorts of trouble, even when they have a loving parent. Best we can do is be there for them, and say lots of prayers."

Wichita's phone vibrated. This time, he didn't pick up the call.

"Oh, Mr. Johnson, another package arrived for you a little while ago. I have it at the front desk."

"Thank you, Coralee."

Another package? I was premature in crossing Wichita's name off the suspect list. He has a few secrets which sound like motive. Did he kill Carter? Perhaps he and Holly worked together. The more puzzling question is how did they do it?

Chapter 11

Henry had been working in the emergency room all morning. Just as he was about to take a late lunch, a new patient came in with chest pains.

"Franklin? What are you doing here? The nurse says you're having chest pains. When did they start?"

"I felt a few twinges this morning, but after lunch it got worse. Coralee's son, Noah, drove me over. He's in the waiting room."

"We're going to run some tests ASAP. Do you have a history of heart problems?"

"Yeah. I've got pills for it but I've gotten a little forgetful about taking them."

"Do you remember the name of the medication?"

"Not really. The bottle's at home. I can get Holly to bring it over."

"First things first. Let's have a listen." Henry pulled up Franklin's shirt. He was surprised to see an odd spider web tattoo covering his chest. "Quite a tattoo. Were you in the military?"

"Nope." He said nothing further and Henry respected his privacy. The orderly came in to take Franklin for testing.

"I'll talk to you after I get back the results." *Should give me a little time to run down to the cafeteria and get something to eat.* He scrubbed his hands in the sink, then went downstairs.

The specials look like they've been sitting out too long. Henry piled his tray with soup, a turkey sandwich, and a slice of cheesecake. The cafeteria was past its lunch rush and Henry didn't see anyone to sit with. He pulled out his tablet while he ate.

I really wonder about that tattoo Franklin has. He wasn't in the military. Was he in a gang when he was younger? Henry googled 'gang symbols,' but didn't recognize any of them. Next he tried 'uncommon tattoos.' Scrolling through them while he ate, he stopped when he found the one Franklin had on his chest. *This is a surprise. I guess Franklin has a secret past. I never heard him mention being in prison before.*

Franklin's spider's web tattoo was pictured along with other 'common prison tattoos.' Henry had been reading books about private investigating ever since his and Emily's friends Susan and Mike had visited and they had all solved a murder together. He had to admit, aside from the fact that someone had lost her life, and that wasn't a small aside, the problem solving aspect had been a lot of fun. He knew which databases the public had access to, and searched prison records. Eventually, Franklin's name popped up.

Well, what do you know? So Franklin Matherson had been arrested and charged with assault with a deadly weapon. He spent years in state prison. You'd never know it by speaking to him. He's a quiet, normal kind of guy. I guess you never know.

When Henry got back upstairs, Franklin's test results were back. He wrapped the stethoscope around his neck and went to his patient.

"How are you feeling?"

"Much better. No more pain. Maybe it was just the stress of my son-in-law's death and having my daughter and grandson living with me. I've been watching my diet and taking my walks."

"The test results look good. I'd suggest being diligent about your pills, though. Might be a good idea to check in with your cardiologist, before you have another episode."

"Thanks, Doc. I'll do that. Gotta be getting back to work."

"I heard you were a chemist before you retired."

"Retired? Try finding a real job with a ...well, let's say I'm thankful to Coralee for hiring me."

Henry wondered if Coralee knew about Franklin's prison record. He'd been working at the inn for a while now and had finished serving his sentence a decade ago. If she'd had problems with him, she wouldn't have kept him on. Coralee's son had served time in prison, so even if she knew about Franklin's record, chances are she'd have given him a break. He wasn't going to bring it up.

The afternoon progressed slowly. Henry's mind drifted to the decision he and Emily would soon have to make. *I think I'd be a good father. I have patience. I could teach Madelyn how to drive and help her pick out a college when the time comes. Maybe we've been missing something by not having children and this was God's way of giving us one last chance.*

Chapter 12

Henry and Emily pulled into their driveway at exactly the same time.

"How was your day with the 'wanna be' writers?" said Henry.

"There's no such thing as a 'wanna-be' writer. If you write, you're a writer. You've heard me say that a million times. They're all improving and I hope they feel it's a worthwhile experience. I know I'm enjoying it. Hope it becomes a yearly thing." She unlocked the front door.

"I found out a little tidbit about Franklin. Did you know he spent time in prison?" said Henry.

"Prison? Hard to picture. What for?"

"Assault with a deadly weapon."

"Really? I never would have imagined it."

Henry kicked off his shoes and flopped down on the sofa. Emily went upstairs and changed into a pair of shorts and a t-shirt. She spotted the letter from the lawyer on her desk.

What are we going to do about this? I'd feel awful putting Madelyn into foster care when Fiona trusted me to be her guardian. On the other hand, it's an overwhelming responsibility, raising a child, especially a teenager. And she'd likely be coping with some heavy grief. How would that affect her behavior? She just lost her mother and here I'd be trying to act as her new mother?

When she came back into the living room, Henry was on the phone.

"Candy? Um, yes, it was supposed to arrive while I was there. Gourmet candy? From the Sugar-Buried Shoppe? Oh yes, the Sugar-Buried Shoppe. Hmm. One of my associates is still in town. I'll have her stop by and pick it up. Thanks for calling."

"What on earth was that about?"

"A box of gourmet candy was delivered to the Ramada Inn for Carter. They had my number, since I registered as Carter. I think a little ride is in order. Feel like playing the part of my business associate?"

"Sure. I'm glad the Ramada is far enough away that Carter's story hasn't been plastered all over the news. No one batted an eye when you said you were Carter Jenson."

"And I pre-paid with a money order, so no checking the name on a credit card."

Henry and Emily hopped into the Audi. On the way, they went around in circles over the custody issue. Emily felt like she was on a teeter-totter. Henry felt like a hamster going round and round on a wheel.

When they arrived at the Ramada Inn, Henry said, "You go in. I'm afraid I might be recognized since I had some interactions with the front desk."

Emily went inside, where she found the clerk flipping through a magazine.

"Good evening. The hotel called my colleague, Carter Jenson, and said there was a box of chocolates that arrived for him."

"Oh, yes." The clerk reached under the desk. "Here you go."

"Gourmet chocolates, huh? Must have had a sweet attack."

"I don't think it was a whim. The Sugar-Buried Shoppe sent chocolates at least two other times while Mr. Carter was here. It stuck out in my mind because those chocolates are handmade and very expensive.

Plus, they charge to send them. Look at that huge box? I love chocolate but I could buy twenty bags of Hershey bars for the same money."

Emily examined the package. She checked the postmark. "Looks like these were supposed to arrive a week ago."

The clerk looked at the box. "They sent it to the wrong Ramada Inn, that's why. Not the first time that's happened."

"Well, thanks for contacting Mr. Jenson. I'm sure he'll be thrilled to have these."

Emily brought the candy to the car. "We have to have these analyzed. It's possible we found our murder weapon. Want to make a bet these are poisoned?"

"Let's drop it off at the police station."

"If we do, they'll never tell us the test results. What if we let Pat Hester have a crack at it, then give them to the police."

"I don't know. Wouldn't that be obstructing justice?"

"Just delaying it. The box has already been handled by the clerks at both Ramada Inns and the mail man. We'll be careful not to add more prints."

"If they are poisoned, someone had to know Carter's routine of ordering these whenever he came to town. They had to at some point have had access to the candy, either at the shop or at the hotel. I'll tell you what. We open the box, take one out, and bring the rest to the police."

Emily grabbed her gloves, which had been in the glove compartment since winter. She carefully opened the box.

"What's that silver pack?" said Henry.

"A cold pack. These could have been a melted mess by now without it." She peered into the box. "Phew. I was worried these might be in individual slots, you know, like Fanny Farmers. They're loose. The police will never know we took one." She carefully wrapped one in the scarf.

Traffic was light. When they got closer to Sugarbury Falls, they noticed a number of walkers and bikers enjoying the evening.

"It's cooler tonight. That little bit of a breeze makes a difference," said Emily.

Soon they were in front of the police station. When they went inside, Detective O'Leary was working at the front counter.

"Mr. and Mrs. Fox. Can I help you?"

"We brought you something. These chocolates were delivered to the Ramada Inn, where Carter Jenson was staying. They arrived late because of a mix-up with the address. The clerk at the hotel said it wasn't the first time Carter had chocolates delivered. They're from a gourmet shop."

"Mrs. Fox, why did the hotel call you about this? How did they even have your number?"

Emily squirmed. *Come on. Think fast.*

"My guess is that they tried to call Carter's cell. When they couldn't, they must have called his office. People at his office knew he was coming up here for my workshop and must have given them my number. These are expensive chocolates we're talking about. Worth tracking down the rightful recipient." She searched the detectives face, hoping she believed her story, but Megan O'Leary had the classic poker face, revealing nothing.

Detective O'Leary took the box. "Thank you for bringing this by."

Once outside the station, Emily said, "I think she bought our story."

"The important thing is that she takes it seriously and rushes it to the lab. Let's drop this other piece by

Pat's. He should be home. He was looking forward to watching the Red Sox game tonight." Henry called and gave his friend a head's up.

They drove over to his cabin. Pat has lost his wife to cancer years earlier but remained in the oversized home they'd shared. Henry knocked, surprised at the response from inside.

"Aww, crap!" Pat flung open the door. He wore a Red Sox jersey and a matching baseball cap.

"I'm sorry. Is this a bad time?"

Pat laughed. "No, of course not. The Red Sox were ahead. It's bottom of the seventh inning and the damn Yankees just got a grand slam!"

"Should we come back later?"

"Nah, get in here. Want a beer?"

"Sure."

"You too, Emily?"

"Just a glass of water is fine."

Pat's place still had a warmth to it, atypical for what was essentially a bachelor pad. *I'd better keep Pat away from Tessa and Maria! They would pounce on him like rabid dogs. On the other hand, I wonder how well he knows Detective O'Leary. She could use a little color on her face, but she's naturally pretty.*

Pat came back in with the drinks, turning the volume down on the Red Sox game. "So where's this poisoned candy?"

Emily fished it out of her purse. "Voila."

Chapter 13

he next morning, Emily left the house with a singular goal. She was determined to talk to Holly. She caught Holly in the parking lot of St. Edward's.

"Good morning, Holly. Are you feeling okay?"

"Hello, Mrs. Fox. Yeah, I'm okay. Still anxious to get Carter buried already. I'm hoping when Jimmy sees his father's body going into the ground, he'll understand he isn't coming back. What are we doing today?"

"We're going to explore point of view. It's important to carefully pick which character's eyes the story is told from. Depending on point of view, the same events can be portrayed very differently."

"Hmm. Like in my story. The single mother thinks the baby daddy is a first class jerk for leaving. If told from the father's point of view, it's painted as a noble act. He sacrifices a relationship with his child so the mother is free to choose a better life for them." She paused. "I'm telling my story through the eyes of the mother."

They walked into the building, Holly sipping coffee from a travel mug.

"You know," said Holly. "Maybe we could add a point of view menu to Story-WOW-ica@."

When she saw Logan coming down the hall, Emily walked slower so she'd have more time to talk to Holly. "That's a great idea. You could even put a tutorial explaining the advantages and disadvantages of each option. In class, I'm going to use a box of candy as an example. From my point of view, it's an irresistible temptation with the potential to blow my diet. From my husband's point of view, it's simply a tasty treat. Men are like that. Was Carter that way too?"

"Carter hated chocolate. All sweets for that matter. I never understood it myself."

So the chocolates weren't for Carter. There had to be a mistress staying somewhere near the hotel. When they reached the classroom, everyone except Wichita was present and ready to work.

Emily began, "Today we're going to talk about…"

Wichita, out of breath, ran into the room and said, "Sorry I'm late." Holly rolled her eyes at him.

Emily didn't miss a beat. "Most of you have chosen a point of view for your story. Maria, yours is in first person, which lets us see how your heroine fears the alpha-leader and yet pushes herself to stand up against him."

Logan said, "Mine is in first person, too. If it were written from the boss's point of view, the reader would experience the story as the boss does and conclude that there's nothing wrong with stealing someone's idea and claiming it as your own. Writing from the employee's standpoint, the reader feels the angst it causes the narrator, and sympathizes with him…even to the point of cheering for the narrator when he murders the boss."

"Great illustration, Logan. All of you go on and choose a page from your work in progress and write it from another character's point of view. After lunch we'll share what you wrote."

The assignment kept the participants busy all morning. At lunch time, Emily stayed back while the others went to the small food court in the student union building. She was dying to call Henry and see if Pat had made any progress on the chocolate. As she walked toward the hallway in search of better phone reception, she spotted an envelope on the ground behind the door.

One of the participants must have dropped this. She crouched down and picked it up. *Hmm. It has Wichita's name on it. It looks official.* She rationalized that since the envelope was already open, it wouldn't hurt to take a peek at the contents. She looked around to make sure she was alone. *Oh, wow. Wichita's house is going into foreclosure if he doesn't catch up on the mortgage in the next thirty days. Poor man. He's working for a successful company. Why is he having financial problems?*

Her phone vibrated. "Hi, Henry. I was just about to call you. Did Pat test the chocolate yet? What? I'm really surprised. No sign of poison?" She told him about Carter not liking sweets and Henry agreed the chocolates must have been meant for a girlfriend. They'd have to go back to the drawing board to figure out the identity of this mystery woman, who hadn't shared Carter's hotel room.

Noticing the time on her phone and the growling sounds from her stomach, Emily decided to run over to the food court and grab a quick lunch. Luckily the line was short. She took her purchase—yogurt and a chocolate chip cookie—outside to eat. Across the courtyard, she had a direct view of Wichita and Holly. Although she couldn't hear what they were saying, their body language spoke volumes.

Look how Holly's flipping her hair and standing so close to him. Wichita keeps finding reasons to touch her as he talks. No way. Could the two of them be romantically involved? So soon after Carter's death?

Logan, Tessa, and Maria came over and sat at Emily's table.

Logan said, "Strawberry yogurt and a cookie. You know, back when I was in school at Chapel Hill that's exactly what I used to buy for lunch, at least on the days when I didn't have time to go to the cafeteria. I remember especially on Tuesdays and Thursdays. I had my computer programming class on one end of the campus, and my business stats class on the other. I'd dart into a little store on campus that I always passed. "

"Looks like I'll be finishing this up on our way to class just like you did," said Emily.

Emily had put Wichita's envelope back on the floor, exactly where she found it. When he and Holly came in, he stopped to pick it up, shoving it into the pocket of his plaid shorts.

Facing her class, Emily rubbed her hands together like an eager squirrel. "Okay, let's share what you wrote this morning."

Tessa, as always, volunteered to go first. Logan followed. The comments from the participants were insightful, and at a higher level than Emily had expected. She was happy to see the progress everyone was making.

On the drive home, Emily tried to focus on the details of the murder case, but her mind drifted to the subject of Madelyn. *Maybe we should meet her first. No, that's a terrible idea. If we meet her and then tell her we won't take her to live with us, how will that make her feel!*

Chapter 14

"Henry, I'm home," called Emily.

He came out of the kitchen with his cellphone to his ear. She grabbed a Diet Coke from the fridge, then went upstairs to change into a comfy pair of shorts. *If Madelyn comes to live with us, she'll have to take the guest room. It already has a queen-sized bed and the furniture is in good shape. We could shop together for a comforter set and new curtains...*

"Emily, are you coming down?"

"I'll be right there." She climbed down the loft ladder. "Who was on the phone?"

"Detective Wooster. The fanny pack belonged to Carter—like we didn't already know that. Anyhow, he wants us to meet him at the Ramada Inn tomorrow and show him the exact path we took, and the location where we found it."

"It will have to be later in the afternoon, when I'm done teaching."

"I told him that. I have to work tomorrow, too."

Emily heard her ringtone and dug her phone out of her purse. "It's my mother."

"Hi, Mom. Yeah, we're still loving it here. The workshop I'm teaching is going well. The workshop. Remember I told you all about it?" *Not that you listen or care about what I say.*

"What? Isn't that kind of quick? You just met him. Didn't his wife just die? Yes, I know. Men tend to remarry quickly. Fall wedding. Yes, the foliage is beautiful then. No, I don't think you should have the wedding in Vermont. All your friends live near you, in New York. The leaves are just as brilliantly colored in New York in the fall. Yep. Talk to you soon."

Henry said, "Let me guess. Your mother found husband number three."

"You got it. If she asks me to be her maid of honor, I swear I'll have to refrain myself from smacking her."

"Did you tell her she may be a grandmother?"

"Yikes, I hadn't even thought of that." *Did he just imply we were taking Madelyn?* "I'm sure my brother Robbie will be calling soon. I think my mother is foolish and impulsive when it comes to men, but Robbie thinks her antics are downright dangerous."

"Do you feel like cooking, or..."

"Yes, let's go to Coralee's. I have no willpower. I've gained ten pounds since we moved here, you know. Even with my running."

"You can order a salad."

Emily laughed. "Yeah, right." They jumped into the Jeep.

Emily hoped it was early enough that the participants from the workshop wouldn't be eating dinner yet. She craved quiet time with Henry, and besides, they had merely half a week left to respond to the lawyer about Madelyn. On the inn porch, around the corner from the lobby door, Emily noticed Wichita talking on his phone. *Why isn't he sitting here in this comfy rocker instead of hiding around the corner?*

"Henry," whispered Emily. "That's Wichita Johnson having a clandestine phone conversation. I think there's something going on between him and Carter's wife, Holly. I think their relationship may be related to Carter's death." She grabbed his hand, and he followed her lead. They hugged the wall, inched their way down, and stopped just shy of the corner. Emily put her finger to her lips, then pointed to her ear, signaling Henry to listen.

Henry whispered, "Can you hear him? I can't make out what he's saying."

"He's saying something about needing more time. He says he'll have it, not to worry."

"Do you think he's talking to Holly?"

"It sounds more like a business call." They both strained to listen. After a few minutes, Wichita put the phone into his pocket.

"Looks like he's finished the call." As Henry started pulling Emily away, he noticed Wichita was walking in the opposite direction from the front of the inn.

Reading his mind, Emily said, "He has the big room on the first floor. The back entrance is closer. Let's see what he does now."

They gave him a few minutes head start, then snuck around to the back. It was drizzling, and none of the guests were outside. Emily pointed to a window, "That's his room."

"And the window is cracked open," said Henry.

They crouched in front of the window. It was silent outside except for the sound of raindrops hitting the porch. Emily peered over the ledge.

"He has about ten different boxes in there. Hard to believe he's doing business from here when there are workers back at the company who can ship out merchandise. Wait. Now he's slitting a box open. Even brought his own box cutter."

Henry carefully looked over the ledge. "He's taking something out. It's a plastic bag. He's opening it."

"Now look at that. He's got his own plastic bag. Looks just like the one he took from the box."

An owl hooted from above them, causing Emily to let out the beginnings of a scream. Henry clamped his hand over her mouth. "Let's get out of here."

Chapter 15

The next morning, Emily's eyes popped open while Henry was still fast asleep, Chester curled up on his legs. She threw on a pair of running shorts, a sports bra, and a singlet. Last night had been a close call. What was she thinking, spying on a suspected murderer, and possible drug dealer?

It was barely light outside when she started her run. *What's Wichita's game? He needs money desperately or he's going to lose his house. What was inside the box and what was the plastic bag for? Drugs? Our rinky-dink post office is surely easier to get drugs through than one in New York City. We don't have trained dogs or even an x-ray machine here like I bet they have there.* In the half darkness, she spotted her neighbor.

"Good morning, Emily," said Kurt. "Down, Prancer."

"Do you walk Prancer this early every day?"

"Usually. I'm up anyway. Saw Franklin out here too this morning. Says he's trying to keep his ticker healthy. He's got a nasty shiner. Says he got into a fight last night."

"A physical fight?"

"You don't get a black eye from hurling words at each other. He didn't go into details."

"I didn't take him for having a trigger temper. Something must have really set him off."

"Guess so." Prancer pulled on the leash. "I gotta finish walking Prancer. Have a nice run."

Emily turned on her music and continued her run. In spite of the heat, she enjoyed being outdoors early in the morning. When she got home, Henry was eating breakfast. She set the newspaper on the table and poured a glass of water.

"Remember we have to meet Detective Wooster later," said Henry.

"I know. Hey, I had a thought while I was running. If it was drugs we saw Wichita handling last night, do you think he used them to kill Carter?"

"I doubt it. Overdoses on illegal drugs like cocaine, bath salts, heroin—they leave damage behind. Pat didn't mention needle marks or any other findings related to a drug overdose. Besides, those drugs show up right away in the initial toxicology report. If Carter was poisoned, the killer was clever enough to use something obscure—something hard to detect."

"What if Carter found out about the drug dealing? Maybe he threatened to go to the police and that gave Wichita motive for murder."

"I don't know. It sounds plausible enough. I've gotta go. See you later this afternoon."

He gave her a kiss. "You stink."

Emily laughed. "I know, I know. I'm headed for the shower now."

Whoever killed Carter had to know which drugs would show up on a lab report. From what I've seen, Wichita isn't all that bright.

At St. Edwards, Emily's topic of the day was setting. She wrote it in giant letters across the dry erase board, then circled it with a flourish.

"Setting is an important choice in making your story work. Tessa has her couple traveling across the country. It's perfect because no one sees her husband every day to notice him getting sicker. Maria, why did you choose to set your story in the city?"

"My protagonist needs places to hide, and access to things she couldn't find in a small town. And having a lot of people around ramps up the tension."

"Very good. Now, all of you, imagine placing your protagonist in a different setting. Write a page or two where your main character lives in a place you once lived. Be vivid in your descriptions—how did it sound, look, smell...."

While the class was writing, Emily's phone vibrated on the desk. "Robbie? Let me go out into the hall. I'm teaching a class."

Robbie was Emily's younger brother. They'd been close growing up, and even closer after their sister had died.

"Yes, Robbie, she called me too...Way too soon... She barely knows this guy. Yes, of course I remember the last guy she dated. The polygamist. And remember the one from the Alcoholics Anonymous meeting? He got arrested for stealing cars...That's a great idea. Go ahead and hire a private investigator. I'll split the cost with you. Tell Kate I said hello, and kiss my niece for me. Take care, love you too."

Emily circulated around the class. When she came to Wichita, she noticed that his knuckles were bruised. *I think I know who gave Franklin that shiner. What would the two of them be fighting about? Holly?* She read over Wichita's shoulder.

"Very nice. Instead of having your main character grow up in rural West Virginia, you have him growing up in Boston. Interesting. When did you live in Boston?"

"I got my masters there at Boston University."

Wasn't he wearing a Harvard t-shirt the other day? Emily went to Tessa next. "That's very clever. You still need to make the husband more or less anonymous, so you have the wife driving from one big city to another. Are they supposed to be in Boston?"

"Yes. I was born and raised there. Probably die there too. Best city in the world."

"Wichita went to school in Boston. The two of you can compare notes."

Tessa turned to Wichita and they exchanged looks.

Are they ticked off because I said to compare notes? Those looks were glares, not smiles.

"Logan, where did you reset this section of your story?"

"You're going to laugh. I wanted a challenge, so I put the spy in a college town in North Carolina."

"Carter went to college in North Carolina," said Holly. "Small world."

At the end of the day, Emily ran home, grabbed a handful of pretzels, and went right back out with Henry to meet Detective Wooster.

Chapter 16

"Mr. and Mrs. Fox, let's start at the beginning. You rented bikes from the back of the hotel, correct?" asked Detective Wooster.

"That's right," said Emily. "We hopped on the bikes and followed the trail, stopping at each rest stop and looking for anything that may have belonged to Carter Jenson."

"When we got to one of the rest areas, I went into the men's room, and saw the fanny pack in the corner. I had a gut feeling it belonged to Mr. Jenson."

Detective Wooster borrowed a golf cart from the hotel, and Emily and Henry climbed in, directing him down the path.

"In here," said Henry, when they reached the rest room. "I found the fanny pack in the corner of the stall, I'll show you."

Detective Wooster took several photos, then they continued on the path, eventually veering off onto the road where Emily had been running.

"I stopped here, looked down, and saw Carter Jenson, right down there." She pointed to the crime scene.

"We checked for fingerprints. Other than yours, Mr. Fox, and Mr. Jenson's, there was a third set," said the detective. "What can you tell me about Franklin Matherson? I'm sure you've seen him working at the Outside Inn."

Emily was startled. Had they found Franklin's prints on the fanny pack? We know he had a prison record, so if they ran it through the database...

"I've seen him at Coralee's. Nice fellow. Coralee thinks highly of him," said Henry.

"His daughter, Holly, is taking my summer workshop. She and her son recently moved in with him. Holly was married to Carter Jenson, but they were having relationship problems," said Emily. She wondered if she should mention what Kurt had told her, about Franklin having a black eye, and how she'd seen bruises on Wichita's knuckles. She hadn't seen the black eye herself, so she decided not to share that piece of information.

Detective Wooster asked, "Do you know if Mr. Matherson worked for other area hotels, such as the Ramada Inn?"

"I doubt it," said Henry. "I know he works full time for Coralee. Can't imagine he'd have time to hold a second job, unless it was a once in a while sort of thing."

The detective drove the cart back to the hotel. "Thank you, both. Call if you find or remember anything else. Have a good evening."

After the detective drove away, Henry suggested to Emily that they have an early dinner at the Ramada restaurant. He hoped they might find out if Franklin had been at the hotel. Franklin took walks. He could have followed the trail from the hotel either by bike or on foot. It was quite a distance from here to the crime scene, so Henry figured it had to have been on bike. They were seated near a window, with a view of the golf course, and ordered burgers and fries. Henry cut the burger and ate it with his fork.

"I wish we had a picture of Franklin," said Emily. "I'd like it show it to a few employees."

"Didn't you 'friend' your students on social media from your author site after they registered?"

"You're right. Let me check Holly's page." She scrolled through her phone while Henry speared his fries. "Bingo. Here's a picture of Jimmy with his grandfather."

They started by asking the waitress if she'd ever seen Franklin.

The waitress answered, "No, I've never see him, but Carly works the breakfast shift most every day. She might have seen him."

She went into the kitchen, and brought out Carly. Emily was hopeful.

"We were wondering if you remember seeing this man here at the hotel. I'm trying to track him down for a book I'm writing."

The waitress looked at the picture, but didn't remember seeing him. "You can check with the front desk boy. Poor kid's been working day and night since he was hired this summer. He often has the early shift."

Emily took the phone over to the desk, keeping Henry out of sight in case the boy remembered him when he masqueraded as Carter. "Excuse me, I'm writing a book and trying to track down this man. Do you remember seeing him here?"

The clerk looked at the picture. "You know, I do. He wasn't a guest here, but he came by early one morning looking for his friend who was staying here. The friend came down to the lobby, and he started yelling at the guy."

"Yelling about what? Do you remember?"

"Yeah. It was weird. He warned the guy about how he'd get custody of his grandson over his dead body. Then he shoved him, and they had a squabble. I called security on them. The poor guest was blindsided. He was all dressed for a bike ride."

"What does it mean to be dressed for a bike ride?"

"You know, bike shorts, those funny shoes that attach to the pedals. Wearing a sports belt."

"Like a fanny pack?"

"Yeah, but the kind runners and bikers use, not the ones you see tourists with."

"What happened when security showed up?"

"The guy in the picture left, and the guest went for his ride."

Emily thanked him, and met up with Henry back at the table. *If the two had a physical squabble, Franklin could have easily grabbed the fanny pack then and gotten prints on it. But did he slip Carter some kind of poison? That would have been tricky. But then again, Franklin was a chemist. He could have chosen a drug that could be transferred through the skin.* She ran it by Henry.

"It sounds pretty far out there, but I did read about transdermal transfer in one of the private eye manuals I've got. I know we sometimes prescribe patches to patients to deliver medication."

"Let's go through what we know. So far, our suspects are Holly; her father, Franklin; and Wichita. Holly stood to lose her son, and lose money, thanks to a pre-nup. She and Carter were having issues. Issues serious enough to cause her to move in with her father. On top of that, Carter's death meant a huge life insurance payout."

Henry added, "Don't forget she lied and said she didn't know Carter was already in town before the workshop started. Kurt heard them arguing in the general store. And she and Wichita share some kind of secret."

Emily grabbed her notepad from her purse. "I need to write this down so I can keep it straight. Wichita and Holly were hiding something from Carter. I saw them flirting with each other during lunch one day. And Wichita keeps taking private cellphone calls and receiving packages."

"Write down how we saw him taking something which looked like drugs out of the boxes," said Henry. "And you found the foreclosure warning so we know he was having financial difficulties, which is puzzling given his position with the company. Oh, and Carter accused Holly of cheating on him. With Wichita, maybe?"

The waitress brought over coffee and a dessert menu. They ordered lemon cake with vanilla ice cream. Emily flipped the page in her memo book.

"Let's keep going. Franklin has a prison record. He had physical run-ins with both Carter and Wichita. He was with Carter the morning he died. He knew Holly was afraid of losing Jimmy and confronted Carter. His motive would have been to protect his daughter and grandson."

"Don't forget we still don't know who Carter ordered the chocolates for. There's someone else in the picture we have yet to identify."

"Where do we go from here?" said Emily, taking the last bite of her cake.

"I read in one of my PI books that discreet surveillance is the way to go once you have a suspect. I think we should start with Wichita."

Chapter 17

Emily was startled awake by the phone vibrating on her night stand. She rolled over and looked at the alarm clock. *It's 5 a.m. Who on earth is calling now?* "Hello? This is Emily Fox."

Henry rolled over and whispered, "Who is it?"

Emily covered the phone and mouthed, "It's Child Services from Chicago."

"I'm here. Yes, that's correct, we were named Madelyn's guardians. What? But we haven't agreed to take her. We have till the end of the week to decide...is she okay? How did you let her get a hold of a bottle of sleeping pills?! Don't you investigate the foster homes before you let a child live there?" She felt the heat rising in her face. "I have to discuss this with my husband. I'll get back to you." She slammed the phone on the night stand.

Henry said, "What was that all about? Did Madelyn try to kill herself?"

"In a word, yes. Stupid agency puts a vulnerable girl who just lost her mother in a foster home where she can get her hands on sleeping pills. Bunch of buffoons. Madelyn is in the hospital but they're releasing her tomorrow. We have to make a decision."

"The decision is either to fly to Chicago and take Madelyn home with us, or let her be placed in another foster home. We've seen the track record the agency has for choosing foster homes!"

"This is a critical time for Madelyn. If we don't take her..."

"The same thing could happen again, only she might succeed next time. You know what we have to do," said Henry.

"I'll call the airline. Meanwhile, we have to get the room ready and stock the kitchen. What do teenagers eat?"

"Purina Teen Chow...I don't know, probably potato chips and pizza."

"I'll google it. Meanwhile, I still have to teach my class. I'll let them go early so we can shop and prepare." She hugged Henry. "I hope we're up to this."

"We're two educated adults who've handled plenty in our lives. How hard can it be?" He kissed her and got ready to go to the hospital. Meanwhile, he made a note to check on Amazon for a book on raising teenagers.

*****

Henry thought about Madelyn the whole way to the hospital. Like he'd told Emily, how hard could it be? She was already fourteen; it wasn't like they'd have to change diapers or hire babysitters. It could be fun having her around. She could work on jigsaw puzzles with them, watch *Jeopardy*, and he'd get to hear a whole new perspective on world problems and politics.

Before starting his shift, he went down to the morgue to see Pat. Pat was in his office, drinking coffee and writing up a report. He had the radio tuned to a pop station. *I wonder if this is the kind of music Madelyn listens to.*

"Henry, what are you doing here in the bowels of the hospital so early in the morning?"

"Hey, buddy, I've got news. If I had a cigar I'd offer it to you. Congratulate me. I'm going to be a father."

"Woah. Congratulations. I guess this means you're going to take in—tell me if I got this right—Emily's college roommate's daughter?"

"You got it. We got a call early this morning. Poor girl was in a foster home and got her hands on some sleeping pills. If we don't take her, it's going to be a downhill slide. She has no one."

"You're doing the right thing. Sometimes I wish Betsy and I would have started a family early on, before she got sick. We talked about it, but kept putting it off and then, of course, it was too late. What's this kid's name again?"

"Madelyn."

"You and I can take her fishing some time. Do you think she plays basketball?"

"I know nothing about her. I'll meet her tomorrow when we go pick her up in Chicago."

"Exciting times. I'm looking forward to meeting her. Not to change the subject, but I was going to call you. I'm taking a new tactic on our investigation. I think Carter was given a drug that screwed with his heart or breathing, but is hard to detect. Something we don't routinely screen for. I made a list and I'm running tests."

"Great. Hope something shows up." Henry noticed the time and realized he'd be late for his shift if he didn't get going. "Thanks, Pat. Let me know what you find out."

Henry ran up the steps to the emergency wing. *How about heart drugs...Franklin has a heart condition. He never told me what pills he was taking. And then there's Wichita. Looked like he had box loads of drugs of some sort. Were any of those legal prescription drugs? Emily and I assumed they were street drugs but there's quite a black market for prescription drugs these days.*

Henry donned his white coat and treated a patient with food poisoning, then another who came in with a killer migraine. After that, things were calm. He looked up Franklin's number.

"Hey, Mr. Matherson. It's Doctor Fox. I was just calling to see how you're feeling. Good, I'm glad to hear that. By the way, did you ever find out the name of the medication your cardiologist prescribed? Really? Okay, let me know after you ask her."

Franklin doesn't know the name of his medication and doesn't have the bottle. Holly picked it up for him weeks ago and he still didn't remember to get it from her. So much for patient compliance. In that case, Holly had access to the medication and had just as much opportunity as Franklin and Wichita to drug Carter. We know Franklin and Holly were here when Carter was killed. We still need to find out where Wichita was and what drugs he has access to.

By mid-afternoon, the hospital was dead quiet, and another doctor was due to take over. Henry decided to use the time to check on Wichita's stash. It was past lunch, so even if Emily's class had decided to eat at the inn, they'd be back at St. Edward's by now.

Coralee was manning the front desk. "Henry, I hear congratulations are in order."

"I'm guessing Emily was here for lunch."

"She was and she filled me on Madelyn. I think it's wonderful that the two of you are giving this girl a chance at a decent life. Her Mama's up there in heaven smiling, you know."

"Well, let's see if she's smiling after Emily and I are done doing this. I need a *Parenting for Dummies* book or something to go by."

"You'll be fine. I told Emily, just call if you need anything. Not that I'm the best example. My own son was in jail for stealing jewelry from my guests."

"And you both got through it. Now he's finishing his degree and he helps you out here all the time."

"They certainly are resilient. Can I get you something to eat?"

"I'll take a sandwich to go. As soon as Emily gets home we've got to get things ready for tomorrow. Coralee, I wanted to ask about one of your guests— Wichita Jonson. You know, the really tall guy who's in Emily's class. He gets a lot of mysterious phone calls, and we've seen him picking up packages here at the desk. Do you think anything funny's going on?"

"Funny how? Like illegal? He does get more mail than any guest I think I've ever had, but he's running a business and now that his boss has died…"

"Yeah, I guess you're right."

"I'll go make you that sandwich. Ham and Gouda on rye?"

"You got it."

While Henry was waiting, the mailman delivered packages to the front desk. One just happened to be addressed to Wichita Johnson. *This is some sort of a sign.* He knew Coralee would be busy a while longer, and the lobby was empty. He noticed a pair of scissors and mailing tape right behind the counter.

Carefully, he slit the package open. He rifled through the Styrofoam noodles and saw a box full of DVDs. *These look legit. Educational DVD's produced by Carter's company.* He dug through the box, under the DVDs. *Voila. Bags of white powder. This has to be cocaine.* He quickly closed the box and resealed it with the mailing tape, right before Coralee came back with his sandwich.

"Thanks, Coralee." Henry spotted a bookcase behind the counter full of souvenirs and gifts. He'd passed it a hundred times, never paying any attention to the individual items.

"Coralee, can I see that stuffed bear? Yeah, the brown one that says *Sugarbury Falls.*"

She handed it to Henry.

"I'll take one of these. How much?"

"A welcome present for Madelyn? See, you have parental instincts. It's on the house."

Chapter 18

"I'm so nervous my knees are shaking," said Emily. Mid-flight enroute to O'Hare, any plans to nap had gone by the wayside. "Do you think she'll like us? Do I look okay?"

Emily had struggled over what to wear for this meeting. She didn't want to look too overdressed, so she nixed the silk wrap-around dress as well as the linen business suit. After trying on every piece of clothing in her closet, she'd decided on a pair of camel-colored dress pants and a summer weight white sweater.

Henry, wearing navy dress pants and a short-sleeved button-down shirt said, "I hate to say it, but she hasn't got a lot of options. Why shouldn't she like us? I'm worried about consoling her over her mother's death. She has to be falling apart over that."

"I read on the internet about the stages she's going to go through. It'll probably take a good six months for her to get over this. Meanwhile, we have to be strong, structured, and supportive. That's what one of the articles said."

When they landed in Chicago, they grabbed their carry-ons and found a taxi. Within a few hours, their lives would be changed irrevocably. Emily fidgeted in the back of the cab. Henry drummed his fingers on the door rest. The cab weaved through city traffic, eventually pulling up in front of a glass building in midtown.

"Here we are," said Henry.

"It's after lunch time. Do you think she ate? Maybe we should take her out for a hamburger or something."

"First things first. Come on." Henry held her hand and they huddled together in the elevator. The secretary was expecting them.

"Have a seat. I'll let them know you're here."

Emily's heart thumped against her chest. She hoped she didn't look as nervous as she felt.

She could tell Henry was nervous by his stiff posture and firmly locked jaw. When the door opened, she felt like she was going to keel over. *Come on feet. Move forward. That's it.*

The lawyer and Child Services representative introduced themselves, but Emily didn't hear a word they said. Her gaze was fixed on the petite, blond girl in the chair in front of the desk. She was younger looking than Emily had imagined her. She looked so fragile sitting slumped in the chair as if trying to make herself disappear.

"Mr. and Mrs. Fox, this is Madelyn," said the lawyer.

Madelyn stood up and awkwardly shook their hands. She had Fiona's blue eyes and rounded nose. She was wearing jeans with threads showing at the knees, not because they were worn out, but because distressed jeans were a hot fashion item. Emily had seen them modeled on *The Today Show*. Emily felt like she should hug Madelyn, but was afraid to.

Henry pulled the bear he'd gotten at Coralee's out of their tote bag. "Here, this is for you. Welcome to Vermont." *That sounds dumb. We're not in Vermont yet.* He hugged her stiffly, and thought he saw a fleeting smile on Madelyn's face. Within an instant, her expression was sullen, eyes focused at the floor.

"We have some paperwork to sign," said the lawyer." He wasn't kidding. Emily's fingers hurt by the time she finished signing and initially not only the paperwork from the lawyer, but also the stack the Child Service's representative required. Then it was Henry's turn to do the same. While Henry was signing, the Child Services rep took Emily back into the waiting area.

"Don't expect it to be smooth sailing. Fourteen year old girls are tough enough under normal circumstances. This one's been through a lot. She'll be starting high school in the fall, which will be another stress added on top of losing her mother and moving halfway across the country. If you need help, we can put you in contact with counselors in your area." She pulled a binder from her oversized purse. "Here. This is some basic information on welcoming a new child into the home."

Does she have all her shots and get a complimentary doctor visit, too? I felt more prepared when we adopted Chester from the shelter. "Thank you. I'm sure we'll be fine."

Henry peeked into the waiting area. "We're done in here. Ready to go? Come on Madelyn." He picked up her suitcase. Her other belongings were being shipped directly to Vermont.

Madelyn reluctantly stood up and in a barely audible voice said, "Maddy. Everyone calls me Maddy."

The three of them rode down the elevator in silence, then got into a cab which was parked in front of the building.

"We thought we'd get some lunch," said Emily. "We passed an Applebee's. Does that sound okay?"

Maddy shrugged her shoulders. "I guess."

Once seated, they scanned the menus. "A cheeseburger sounds good to me," said Henry. "Do you like burgers?"

Maddy looked at him with steely eyes. "I don't eat dead carcasses."

Startled, but trying to stay calm, Emily said, "So you're a vegetarian. You should have told us. I know we passed pizza places. Do you eat cheese?"

"I'm vegetarian, not vegan, but I won't eat eggs that aren't from cage-free chickens. As far as milk goes, only Almond or Soy. This will be fine."

When the waitress came, Maddy ordered a plate full of fries with a side of guacamole. Emily's head was spinning, going through the handful of vegetarian dishes she could make. Quesadillas, tofu stir fry, veggie burgers…too bad she wouldn't be able to impress Maddy like she did everyone else, with her famous chicken cacciatore or her double baked pot roast casserole. She could still whip up her delectable caramel brownies. Did they sell cage-free eggs at the general store or would she have to order them from Amazon?

"So, Maddy, do you like sports?" asked Henry.

"I think they're stupid."

"What do you like to do in your free time? We live near a lake, if you like swimming or boating. Our neighbors have their own jet ski."

"I don't know how to swim."

The waitress set the food on the table. Henry wondered if it bothered Maddy that he was eating a dead cow in front of her. Too bad if it did, he was starving. Maddy picked at her fries.

Emily said, "There's a dance studio in town if you want to take lessons. And we have a piano, though I haven't played in years. It belonged to Henry's mother. If you like art, we can buy some painting supplies."

"No thanks. I brought some books with me. I can entertain myself."

After lunch, they checked into the hotel. Feeling awkward about being in the same bedroom, Henry had found a place with suites. Maddy closed her bedroom door and didn't come out until it was time to get dinner. Meanwhile, Emily read through the binder from child services, and asked the front desk for pizza parlor recommendations.

When it was time for dinner, they settled into a booth at Giovanni's Pizza. Emily slid in next to Maddy. The tables in the center were covered with red and white checkered cloths and the waitresses wore cheerful green aprons. Their place settings were on top of placemats shaped liked Italy. The conversation was stiff, and mostly one-sided.

"So what kind of music do you like?" asked Henry.

"You wouldn't know it," said Maddy.

"We can go watch a movie tonight after dinner," said Emily. "Would you like that?"

"No. I'm really tired."

Maddy gazed down at her pizza, avoiding eye contact. Dinner was as awkward as lunch had been, with the three of them finishing their meals in silence. Emily normally loved eating out, but was relieved when this meal was finished. Was it going to be like this from now on?

Back at the hotel, Emily and Henry closed the door to their bedroom.

"I think she hates us," said Henry.

Trying to convince herself as much as Henry, Emily said, "No, I read that's how teenagers act. Maybe we're trying too hard. Tomorrow we'll take her home and give her some space. We're both working. She'll have to find ways to entertain herself. She told us she knew how to do that."

"I don't know. I'm already feeling like this wasn't such a good idea."

"She just needs time. I think she'll fall in love with Sugarbury Falls."

"Who doesn't know how to swim? That's the first thing we have to do is get her swimming lessons. It's a safety issue. All we need is to have her drown."

"I'll ask Coralee about it. And Henry, I was thinking…"

"Thinking what?"

"How would you feel about raising cage-free chickens?"

Chapter 19

Back in Vermont, Emily woke up early to make breakfast, grateful it was the weekend. She hadn't run in a few days and her body was feeling it. She opened the front door and picked up the newspaper, then she opened the fridge door and stared at the shelves. *If I stick with pancakes, I'll be safe. Everyone likes pancakes.* She mixed fresh blueberries into the bowl and poured the batter on the griddle, ignoring the fact that the eggs she'd used as well as the milk were most likely unacceptable. *If she's hungry, she'll eat.* She heard Henry climbing down the loft.

"Is she up yet?" asked Henry. He grabbed a cup of coffee and sat down at the table.

"No. I read that teenagers sleep late. Plus, she's probably exhausted from the trip. We got home pretty late. I've got our breakfast going. I'll put the rest in the fridge until she wakes up."

She flipped the pancakes, put out the butter and syrup, and then brought the golden stack to the table.

Henry said, "I didn't want to get into it with our minds on Maddy the other day, but I found out two things about Carter's murder. First, Pat says he's pretty sure it was some kind of medication overdose that killed Carter. Something undetectable that threw his system off and killed him. Franklin is on medication for his heart, though I'm not sure how often he remembers to take it. Holly picked up his last prescription, meaning they both had access to it."

"And they were both in town at the time."

"The other thing I found out, was it was definitely white powder Wichita was unpacking the other night. I'm almost sure it's cocaine. It was packed in a box under a bunch of DVDs made by Carter's company."

"How did you find that out?"

"I went by the inn after work the other day. I saw a box addressed to Wichita on the front counter, so I opened it up, had a look, and then resealed the box."

"You didn't!" She knew she should be horrified that he'd committed a crime by tampering with the mail, but instead she felt kind of proud.

"The cocaine didn't kill Carter. Pat says they screen for street drugs routinely in an autopsy. He was slipped a lethal dose of some medicine. I was thinking about the candy. I looked on-line and found the address of the shop. It may be worth taking a ride over there and seeing if they ever met Carter, and if they have any idea who he sent the candy to."

Emily's phone vibrated. "Hello, Coralee. Yes, it went just fine. She's sleeping now. Coralee, one of my students, Wichita Johnson, has been acting rather strangely in class. Have you noticed anything odd about his behavior around the inn? That's right, the tall one...Really? Hmm. I thought there might be something going on between them. We'll come by for dinner later so you can meet Maddy. By the way, she's a vegetarian."

Henry said, "What was that all about?"

"Coralee saw Wichita out on the porch with Holly late last night. It looked like they were having a serious discussion. Then, get this. They kissed. Not just a peck on the cheek, Coralee described it as a *romantic* kiss. I knew there was something going on. It sounds like Carter knew she was cheating on him. Do you think he knew it was with Wichita? Do you think he confronted or even threatened him?"

"Threatened him so that Wichita felt he had to kill him? Hmmm. With Carter out of the way, the path is clear for him and Holly. What else did Coralee say?"

"She heard him arguing with someone on the phone. He looked scared and asked Coralee what other hotels were in the area."

Maddy walked into the kitchen. In a shy voice, she said, "Good morning."

Both Henry and Emily, too enthusiastically, returned the greeting. Maddy took a step backward. Emily took a deep breath and slowed down.

"I made pancakes with blueberries and we have locally made maple syrup. Sit down and I'll get you some." Emily took the batter out of the fridge and turned the griddle back on. "Did you sleep well?"

"Yeah, I guess. Where's Chester?"

"He's probably under the bed. Would you like to feed him? As soon as you pop open the can of cat food watch him come running. Here, chicken is his favorite." Maddy crinkled her nose. Surely she didn't expect the cat not to eat meat. She handed the can to Maddy and pointed to the food bowl.

Henry said, "We'd like to show you the town after breakfast. Tonight we'll go to the Outside Inn for dinner. It's quintessential Sugarbury Falls."

"And we can drive out to the outlet shops and pick up a nice comforter and curtains for your room. You can make it your own."

Maddy nodded.

"There's soap and shampoo in the downstairs bathroom, but if you prefer a different brand we can pick that up too."

Maddy picked at the pancakes. "What are you doing?" she asked Henry. He was sitting across from her with the newspaper and a pen in front of him.

"It's Sudoko. It's a number puzzle. See, you can only use each number once in each part."

Maddy seemed mildly interested in watching Henry work on it. She ate about half of her pancakes, then got up to take a shower.

"You know," said Emily, "isn't the candy shop out by the outlet mall?"

"It sure is." Henry's phone rang. "It's Pat."

Emily cleaned up the breakfast dishes while Henry talked.

"They did? That narrows it down. So it was in the gel packs? Injected into them? Pretty sophisticated, don't you think? It's time I find out what Franklin was taking. Yeah, she's doing okay. I don't think she'll care about shooting hoops, though. The girl hates sports. Talk to you later."

Emily closed the dishwasher. "They know what poisoned Carter?"

"Yes, the police came by the hospital and asked Pat if he could test for a heart drug called Digoxin. It's not typically screened for in an autopsy. The energy gel packs that were in the fanny pack were laced with it, and apparently there were tiny needle holes. This was well planned and could have been done days, even weeks ahead of time."

"Someone had to have access to the gel packs, and a hypodermic needle. Don't you need a prescription for needles?"

"Yes, but needles have an infinite shelf life. Too hard to trace. And Franklin couldn't have burst into the Ramada Inn, gotten into a scuffle with Carter, and managed to inject the pack during that interchange."

"But he could have done it a different day."

"Yes, and it widens the suspect pool knowing the energy gels could have been tampered with before Carter even arrived in Vermont."

Chapter 20

The drive to the outlet store took them past the lake and into the foothills of the mountains, famous for attracting skiers and packing the lodges in the area to capacity during the winter. Summer promotions kept business going year round. The ground was jewel green, lush with trees. In addition to several area lakes, every lodge had its own pool and hot tub. Henry had taken Emily here for a surprise anniversary weekend once. Rounding a bend, he pulled into an oversized strip mall.

"These outlet stores are one of this area's biggest tourist attractions," said Emily. "This store over here has really nice linens and quilts. When we first moved here this is where I bought the one for our bedroom."

Madelyn and Henry followed Emily's lead, winding through rows of sheets, culminating in a bin full of comforter sets.

"What colors do you like, Maddy?"

"I don't know." She sifted through the bin, lifting out a mint green and lavender printed set. "This is kind of nice."

"Oh, I love it," said Emily. She knew she was being overly enthusiastic again—trying too hard to get Maddy to like her. She'd have to lay back or she'd scare the poor girl off.

"What about this one?" said Henry, holding up a blue paisley set.

"I think I like the green one better," said Maddy. Henry was glad she felt comfortable enough to assert an opinion. Maddy went to the next aisle and browsed through the sheet sets.

"This matches," said Emily. "Why don't you pick out two or three that you like."

Henry turned around and literally ran into Holly. "I'm sorry. I was so absorbed in sheet patterns, I didn't see you behind me."

Holly was wheeling a shopping cart with Jimmy sitting up front. "I came to get some new sheets and a bedspread for Jimmy. He graduated out of a toddler bed; isn't that right, Jimmy? You're a big boy now."

"That Superman bedspread you've got in the cart looks pretty cool to me." Jimmy smiled at him. "Holly, I want you to meet someone. This is Maddy. She's going to be living with us from now on."

"Hi, Maddy. I'll bet you'll love it here. I moved here from New York recently and am enjoying the Vermont charm. Do you babysit?"

Maddy shrugged her shoulders. "I never did but I guess I could."

Emily called Maddy into the next aisle. While he had her alone, Henry asked Holly about her father's heart medication.

"It's some sort of generic beta blocker. He's been taking it for years."

"Not Digoxin, is it?"

"No, I'm sure that isn't it."

"I think I already asked, but did Carter take any heart medications?"

"No. With all the biking he did, he was healthy as a horse."

Emily called to him from the next aisle. "I'll be right there!" Henry yelled back. He bent down to Jimmy's eye level. "Enjoy your new Superman set."

When the three of them were back in the Jeep, Henry pulled out the directions to the candy shop.

"Thank you for the stuff," said Maddy. She stuck her earphones in and fiddled with her phone. They pulled onto the main road.

"Maddy, do you like chocolate?" said Emily. She didn't get an answer. "Maddy, I said do you like chocolate?"

"She can't hear you," said Henry. "She's got her earphones in."

Emily turned around to the back seat and motioned to Maddy to take out the earphones. Then she repeated her question.

"Huh? As long as it's domestic, or it comes from a country that fairly compensates its workers."

Henry said, "All they've got is domestic, I'm sure. They make it right in the store." He pulled in front of the shop.

The aroma of chocolate gave Emily an endorphin rush. The store had a little factory in the back with a glass window for customers to watch the candy being made. Maddy pressed her face near the glass. "I like chocolate with macadamia nuts the best."

Emily figured with the dozens of varieties the store carried, that would be the one type they wouldn't have. She was pleasantly surprised when the owner said they carried it. *I thought kids liked plain chocolate, or maybe chocolate with peanut butter. Macadamia nuts?*

Henry took the owner aside. "A friend of mine was a regular customer here. He ordered a box of chocolates for his wife each month over the past few months. Unfortunately, he's passed away. I'd like to continue sending them to his wife if you'd be so kind as to look up the information."

"I'm so sorry to hear that. Let me look him up. What's his name?"

"Carter Jenson."

"Jenson…here it is. Few months? He's been sending our candy to the same address every month for years."

"Can I get the address?"

"Sometimes we sent it over to the Ramada Inn, but mostly we mailed it to Sweet Water Manor. To an Ellie Jenson. Is that his wife?"

Henry felt confused, but said, "Yes, that's her."

"Here's the address."

"Sweet Water Manor. Is that the name of a town?"

"No, it's a long-term care facility. One of the nicest in the state from what I hear."

"Thanks."

Emily and Maddy carried a metal tray full of assorted candies. With waxed paper, Henry grabbed a handful of peppermint bark, added it to the mix and brought it to the register. *Sweet Water Manor. His wife?* He couldn't wait to tell Emily.

Chapter 21

Emily bubbled as she walked into Coralee's with Henry and Maddy. She was going out to eat with her *family*, not just her husband. Hoping they were over the initial awkwardness of their first restaurant experience, she looked forward to introducing Maddie to her friends. Maddy looked fashionable in her new jeans and handkerchief-styled shirt they'd picked up at the American Eagle Outlet earlier. Her blond hair was pulled into an intricate French braid, which impressed Emily to no end. Emily couldn't even make a regular braid without wisps of hair poking out. Her sister used to beg Emily to let her to do it, but it never turned out right.

"Coralee, this is Maddy. Maddy, Coralee Saunders. She owns this bed and breakfast and wait till you taste her cooking."

"I pulled out some vegetarian recipes and put them on the menu. I'd been meaning to do that anyway. Every now and then I'll have a guest who asks about it." She seated them at a round table in the center of the dining room.

At an adjacent table, Emily noticed an oddly-dressed man eating by himself. During the summer, guests typically dressed casually—jeans or, more often, shorts. This bearded gentleman wore a three-piece suit. On a Saturday night. Something felt off about him.

Henry said, "Look, Maddy. Coralee added vegetable lasagna to the menu, a baked squash casserole, and a tofu stir fry. I might try one of those myself."

"Save room for dessert," said Emily. "Coralee could win an award for her apple strudel."

Wichita and Holly appeared at the doorway of the dining room. Coralee led them to a table next to Emily and her family, but Wichita looked around the room. When he saw the stranger in the suit, he fidgeted and whispered something to Coralee, who then led him and Holly to the opposite side of the dining room.

"I wonder what that was about?" said Emily. "I wanted to introduce them to Maddy."

"We'll go by their table later," said Henry. "Maybe he doesn't want you to see him having dinner with Holly."

Emily pointed out all the people she knew to Maddy. "Over there, helping Coralee, is her son, Noah. And by the window, those are our neighbors, Kiki and Buzz. They're pretty irritating. Young and spoiled, both of them. Not that being young means being spoiled. I didn't mean that..." She felt her face flush.

The waitress brought three steaming hot servings of vegetable lasagna to the table. She refilled their drinks and set down a second basket of rolls. "Be careful, the plates are hot. Can I get you anything else?"

"Not right now," said Emily. "This smells delicious." All three dug in.

"Do you like it?" said Henry to Maddy."

"Yeah. It's really good." For the first time since they'd met her, Maddy finished every bite on her plate. Emily took it as a sign she was starting to feel more comfortable.

While they were waiting for dessert, Franklin walked into the dining room. He went directly to Wichita and Holly's table and started yelling. People turned to look, and Wichita followed Franklin out to the lobby.

The waitress brought apple strudel to the table and poured coffee for Emily and Henry.

Emily said, "Poor Holly is sitting there all by herself. I don't think Wichita is coming back. Do you mind if I invite her to sit with us?" Both Henry and Maddy shook their heads.

Emily brought Holly over. "Holly, you remember Maddy from the linen store."

The waitress brought Holly's plate to the table.

"Of course. My future babysitter. Thanks for inviting me to sit with you. Wichita and my father act like children when they're in the same room together. Jimmy shows more maturity than either one of them."

"What were they fighting about?" Emily sipped her coffee. This wasn't the first conflict between those two that Emily had witnessed.

"I was going through the company expense reports for the past few months. Now that Carter's gone, I want to make sure I understand where everything is at. Dad came in and started reading over my shoulder. Wichita had made large deposits to a company called Johnson, Inc. Dad right away jumped to the conclusion that the money was going straight to Wichita."

"I'd be upset, too," said Henry. "Look at it from his point of view. His daughter is now full owner of a company and a supposedly trusted business associate has been stealing money?"

"It looks that way, but that's not what was happening. Wichita was always trying to impress Carter with his next big idea. Carter was always knocking down his ideas and belittled him terribly. Matha-WOW-ica@ made billions. Story-WOW-ica@ is about to launch and is expected to be an even bigger hit. Wichita had developed his own brainchild."

"What was that?" said Emily.

"Dino-WOW-ica@. Wichita funneled money from the company to develop his new project. He surprised Carter by making a prototype and revealing it at the National Educator's Convention in Rochester a few months ago. It's the biggest trade show there is for educational materials. He expected Carter to be thrilled and proud that he'd developed it all on his own."

Henry said, "And was he?"

"Not at all. Dino-WOW-ica@ was received extremely poorly by the convention participants. Carter was furious, saying Wichita was so stupid to think it would be a hit. Then he berated him for wasting all that money developing it."

"If the other two programs had been so popular, why not this one?" said Emily.

"First of all, there are millions of resources and games out there about dinosaurs. Second of all, kids don't care about dinosaurs so much anymore. Thirdly, it had some major design flaws."

"Is she right about kids not caring about dinosaurs anymore?" Emily was talking to Maddy, but realized Maddy had her phone out and her earphones in. She got closer and spoke louder. "Maddy!"

Maddy jumped, then took out the earphones. "What?"

"I was asking you a question. Don't you think it's rude to use your phone like that during dinner?"

"We're done eating, and what's the problem? Mom never cared if I took out my phone."

Emily anticipated the next part would be 'you're not my mother and you can't tell me what to do.' She took a deep breath and held her tongue.

Henry said, "That was a wonderful dinner. I'm stuffed. How about I pay the bill and we take a walk around the golf course so I can get in some steps? I'm third in my Fit-Bit group at the moment. That simply won't do."

Maddy rolled her eyes at him, taking him by surprise.

"Or, we can go home," said Henry.

Chapter 22

Back to work today. Just a summer job and adding a child to the mix turns it from fun to stressful. The bathroom needs cleaning and I never made it to the grocery store. I don't know how working mothers do it. I'll have to get things running more smoothly before the fall semester starts.

Emily strapped on her running watch and headed out the front door. As much as she wanted to hop in her Audi and drive to Sweet Water Manor, she'd have to wait for Saturday. Who was Carter sending candy to every month? Having a clandestine mistress in a long-term care facility didn't seem worth the effort. Was it another wife?

"Hey there, Emily. How's it going with the kid?" said Kurt. Prancer, on his leash, followed Kurt's order and sat beside him.

"It's going. Before you know it, I'll need to register her for Sugarbury High. As a matter of fact, I'd better find out what school she was at before and have her records sent."

"I was going to stop by later. I saw a stranger knocking at your door while you were out over the weekend. He had a beard and he wore a suit and tie. At first I thought maybe he was one of those Jehovah Witnesses, but when he saw me and Prancer, he started asking questions."

"What sort of questions?"

"Wanted to know if I knew a Wichita Johnson. I didn't give him any info. Then he wanted to know if I knew when you'd be home. Again, I said I didn't know."

"Then what?"

"He got into a little black sedan and drove off. I kept watch on your place the rest of the day, just in case. Stranger comes into town like that asking questions, I figure he's up to no good."

"Thanks, Kurt. I feel safer knowing we have our own one-man neighborhood watch unit."

"You'd do the same for me. Didn't mean to hold up your run. See you later."

Emily turned on her music and ran down the road. *That has to be the weirdo in the three-piece suit we saw eating dinner by himself at Coralee's. Wichita didn't want to sit near him. Why did Wichita want to avoid him? Did he borrow money for his Dino-WOW-ica@ project from this guy?*

She didn't know why that thought immediately jumped into her head. She let her mind wander from making a grocery list to finding a pediatrician. Henry would know who was good. A psychologist too. After all, Maddy had tried to kill herself. She finished her run and got ready for work. When she arrived, her students were seated and waiting to start.

"Well, how was your trip?" said Tessa. "Holly told us a little about Maddy."

"We're still getting used to each other, but I think everything will be just fine."

"It seems like a good place to raise a child," Tessa continued. "Back in Boston, the schools have gotten so crowded. They weren't so bad when my son was there, but from what I hear, those who can afford it are choosing private schools over public."

"Tessa, I didn't know you had a son," said Emily.

Tessa bit her bottom lip and balled her fists, tightly. "I *had* a son. He's no longer alive. A drunk driver ran him over in broad daylight. I've never gotten over it. The driver fled town and they never found her. I'm so angry to this day. That woman should be sitting in prison right now. Instead, she's probably living on a beach in Puerto Vallarta"

"Tessa, I'm so sorry. That's horrible."

Wichita said, "That's Boston for you. Could be any big city I guess. Everybody's in a hurry and it's easy to disappear into the crowd."

Logan said, "It's obviously a painful subject. Maybe writing about it would help."

"Speaking of writing," said Maria, "I think we should get to work." She put her arm around Tessa. In spite of their rivalry over Franklin, the two had become close, and Emily realized she was trying to change the painful subject.

Emily said, "Today's topic is conflict. There needs to be conflict or the story drags. Even if you have conflict in your works in progress, let's think about how you could add more. Who wants to start?"

Logan raised his hand. "My protagonist is in conflict with the boss who stole his idea."

"But the boss doesn't know there's a conflict, right?" said Emily. "It's more an internal conflict which is quite valid, but can you add to it?"

"I could have him confront the boss before he kills him. Or he could discuss killing the boss with a trusted friend, or a wife who tries to talk him out of it."

"That sounds like something you may want to explore," said Emily.

"I've got a conflict for you," said Wichita. Emily was happy that he was volunteering. Most of the summer he'd been a quiet observer. "My guy goes to his boss with a great idea, but the boss tells him it's idiotic. He tries to convince the boss that his idea is a money maker, but keeps getting shot down. There are verbal arguments which eventually result in the boss firing him."

From what I've learned, his book sound more like an autobiography than a work of fiction.

*****

Henry had barely donned his white coat when he heard a nurse frantically calling his name.

"Dr. Fox, over here. They're bringing in a little boy who fell out of a tree. He's not breathing."

Henry ran to meet the stretcher. A distraught Franklin was with the boy.

"Henry, you've gotta help him. I didn't know he could climb! We were outside and I swear I looked away for a second and Jimmy was up in the tree. I yelled 'come down right now' but he froze. Then he started climbing down and the whole branch fell off with him on it. Holly's going to kill me. Is he going to be okay?"

"Franklin, I need to focus on Jimmy. The nurse will show you where to wait and there are forms to sign. Call your daughter and get her in here."

Henry and the emergency room staff huddled over Jimmy. "Get ortho down here to look at his leg. The wrist looks broken, too." Henry and his team worked on Jimmy, whose heart stopped twice. "There's internal bleeding. We're going to need blood. He needs a transfusion. Type and match him."

A nurse came into the treatment room. "His mother is here. Can you speak to her?"

"I'll be out in a few minutes." When Henry was confident that Jimmy was stable, he went to the waiting room where Franklin was pacing, and Holly was crying.

Holly noticed him first. "Is he okay? Dad said he wasn't breathing and his leg...can I see him, please?"

"In a minute. We've got him stabilized but he needs a transfusion. His blood type is rare—AB negative. We may not have enough in the blood bank."

"I'll give you blood. I'm type A and his father was type O. Of course his father can't be of any help now."

"You have type A? And Carter had O? Are you sure?"

"I'm positive. What's the problem?" said Holly.

Franklin said, "I'll volunteer, too."

Henry said, "It doesn't make sense. Jimmy can't have type AB if you and Carter had those two blood types. In fact, it's impossible."

Holly looked at the floor. Franklin said, "Holly, what's going on here? Carter was Jimmy's father, right? I was at the hospital when he was born so I know you're his mother."

Henry said, "Franklin, go over to the blood bank and have them type you. Holly, you can see Jimmy now."

"Let me make a quick call first, in case you need more blood." She stepped outside for less than a minute, then followed Henry into the treatment room. Jimmy was awake, but crying.

"Jimmy, baby. Mommy's here now. You're going to be alright." She hugged him, careful not to pull on the IV or monitors.

"When the swelling goes down, he'll get a cast on his leg and wrist. Once he has the transfusion he'll perk up. Carter wasn't his father, am I right?"

"You are. I'm so ashamed. My father didn't know. Even Carter didn't until shortly before he died. His real father will be here shortly if you still need the blood."

"If he's a match, we might need it. There's was a boating accident last week and I know our supplies are low."

"You must think I'm terrible."

"I'm not judging you, Holly. You shouldn't judge yourself either."

Holly sat with Jimmy, now in the pediatric ward, until he fell asleep. She didn't let go of his hand. He wasn't in pain, thanks to the medications he'd been given. Franklin sat next to her, reading part of a newspaper he'd found in the waiting room. His blood type wasn't a match for Jimmy either.

Wichita came in. "Holly, is he doing okay? I just gave blood. They said it was a match."

Franklin stood up, nose to chin with Wichita. "You? You're his father? You bas...."

"Dad, stop. It's a good thing he's here. Jimmy might need the extra blood."

"Holly, how could you carry on with this man? We raised you in a good Christian home and you go and have an affair? And lie to your husband about it? Is that why Carter was going to fire him, or was it about the money he was stealing from the company?"

A nurse opened the door. "Keep your voices down. There are sick children here."

Holly apologized for all of them, and the nurse closed the door on her way out. "What's past is past. Jimmy is still your grandson and we have to keep a united front, especially now that he's lost the man he thought was his father, and he's lying in a hospital bed."

Chapter 23

Henry was sitting at the kitchen table, finishing the Sudoku puzzle he'd started in the morning, when Emily got home. She couldn't wait to hear the details of what had happened. Henry filled her in.

"I'm glad it wasn't worse," said Emily. "The poor little boy. Holly was frantic when she got the call. Sometime later, Wichita got a call and he rushed off to the hospital. What was that all about?"

"Ready for this? Turns out Jimmy needed blood and the hospital was low on his type. Then Holly tells me her blood type, and Carter's, and I say to her…" Henry looked at the sofa, noticing Maddy reading with Chester snuggled next to her. "Um, I'll tell you later."

Maddy stood up. "I'm not a little kid. You can talk in front of me. Believe it or not, I even know about how married people sometimes have affairs. Ooh. And sometimes they even get pregnant. I know all about the birds and the bees so you can cross that lecture off your list."

Taken aback, but keeping a calm exterior, he said, "You can cut the sarcasm, Maddy." He turned back to Emily. "Yes, that's what happened. Holly had an affair, or at least a one-night stand, slept with her husband's business associate, got pregnant, and let her husband believe he was the baby's father."

"See," said Maddy. "I'm not even blushing." She flopped back down on the couch, arms folded. She'd scared the cat away with her ranting.

Emily said, "Maddy, why don't you go wash the lettuce that's in the fridge. I'm going to change my clothes and we'll make dinner."

Henry followed Emily into the bedroom. "Should we let her talk to us like that?"

"It's probably better to ignore it. So what happened at the hospital?"

"Franklin was blindsided. He obviously thought Carter was Jimmy's father. He was already mad at Wichita because he thought he was stealing from the company."

"This is worse than a soap opera," said Emily. "Do you think we can take a ride to Sweet Water tomorrow after I get home? I'm dying to see how this piece of the puzzle fits in. I hope whoever was at the receiving end of that expensive candy can shed some light on it."

"You think Maddy will be okay alone for a few hours at night?"

"She'd probably enjoy the space. Besides, if she's old enough for Holly to ask her about babysitting, surely she can stay by herself."

When they went into the kitchen, Maddy was clumsily cutting the lettuce with a serrated knife. Henry washed his hands and said, "Here, you can just tear it, like this." He wondered if Fiona had spent any time cooking with her.

Emily boiled water for the linguine. Then she proudly opened a Mason jar full of tomato sauce, which she'd canned earlier in the summer under Coralee's tutelage. There were enough jars full of sauce in the pantry to get them through till Christmas. Thank God she hadn't added meat.

"Maddy, what did you do while we were gone today?" asked Emily.

"I read and watched TV, and took a nap. The usual."

"I'm going to look into swimming lessons for you. That will be fun," said Emily.

"Fun for who? I don't want to get my hair full of chlorine. I can entertain myself." She continued tearing the lettuce.

Henry's phone vibrated. It was the hospital. "Great, I'm glad to hear it. You can up the pain meds if he needs more to get him through the night. I'm sure his mother is glad he's out of the woods. Tell her I'll talk to her in the morning."

"Sounds like Jimmy is doing better," said Emily.

"Much better. He didn't wind up needing the blood transfusion after all and he actually ate some dinner. After the swelling goes down, he'll get his casts and he can go home."

"I guess Franklin won't be able to work. Or Holly will have to quit my class. They can't send him to Tiny Tots in the shape he's in."

Maddy looked up from her plate. "I can watch him. His mother already asked if I wanted to babysit."

Emily said, "I'll check with his mother. What a nice offer."

Henry said, "I almost forgot. Another box came for you, Maddy." He carried it to the coffee table. "Do you want me to open it for you?"

"Yes."

Henry got a knife from the kitchen and opened the heavy box. Maddy looked inside.

"It's photo albums. Me and my Mom." She took them out one by one. "And this is my baby book."

Emily sat next to her and watched as she flipped through the pages. "You were a beautiful baby. Now you're a beautiful young lady." She turned the page. "Look how happy your Mom is holding you. Her whole face is glowing."

Maddy covered her face with her hands and cried. Emily wasn't sure what to do. She awkwardly put her arms around Maddy and said, "I know you miss her. I know this is hard on you. It's okay to cry." She held Maddy for a long time. It broke her heart to see how distressed Maddy was. She understood that losing your mother is difficult, but seeing a daughter's raw emotion first hand broke her heart. At that moment, all she wanted to do was to make Maddy feel better.

Chapter 24

In the morning, Emily checked on Maddy before leaving. She was sleeping curled up with Chester. During the day, she called three times to check on her, noting a growing tone of annoyance on the other end of the line.

After the workshop, Emily quickly changed into a pair of capris and a cotton blouse, gave Maddy dinner instructions, and hopped into the Jeep beside Henry. The ride to Sweet Water Manor took them around the lake and out past the outlet mall.

"My students were sweet to me. When I said I was going to investigate my own real life mystery after class, they agreed to give up their afternoon break and end early."

"The word mystery must have been tantalizing to a bunch of writers. I'm sure they were feeling a little off because of Jimmy's accident, too."

She had to admit that having Maddy even for such a short time had made her empathy for mothers—her own not included—blossom. The little crying incident last night had twisted her stomach in knots. She couldn't stand seeing Maddy hurt and not being able to fix it. All her life, Emily had been a problem solver, but last night she was helpless. *Imagine how Holly feels seeing her little boy in pain.*

She turned to Henry. "How was Jimmy today?"

"The swelling is going down. He's grumpy, but that's understandable. It must be hard for a three year old boy to be confined to bed all day. Once the casts are on, he'll get to start moving a bit. According to the nurses, Holly hasn't left his bedside at all. Franklin's been there most of the time, too."

"Did Wichita stop by at all? He left the workshop at lunch time."

"I didn't see him, but I hope he has the sense to stay away from Franklin for a while. Franklin looked like he wanted to kill him after he found out he was Jimmy's father."

"Do you think Wichita knew? Do you think he acted surprised? And did Carter suspect?"

"If they were smart, Holly and Wichita would have kept this secret close to the vest. Jimmy stands to inherit the company one day, let alone whatever trust fund Carter put together."

"But now that Franklin knows, do you suppose he'll come forward with the information, or keep quiet? Keeping quiet would be the best thing for Jimmy, and we know Franklin adores that boy."

Emily checked her phone for messages while Henry drove—just in case Maddy needed something. Out the side window, she noticed a black car which she remembered seeing when they'd first started out. Was it following them?

"We're almost there. Hope we don't show up when they're all in the middle of dinner."

"Henry, look in the mirror. That black car has been behind us since we left. I think it's following us."

"I see it, but following us? For what reason? Give your mystery-writing brain a rest for now."

They pulled up in front of a two-story, brick building which sat on a small hill. The shutters were painted white, and a wooden sign out front read 'Welcome to Sweet Water Manor.' Having gotten in his steps for the day, Henry pulled into a parking spot right outside the front entrance.

Henry and Emily approached the front desk. Henry signed the visitor's sheet for both of them, while the aide snapped photos for the sticky-backed ID badges.

"Mrs. Jenson's room is on the second floor. She gets tired easily these days."

"Thank you," said Emily. "We won't stay long." The halls were painted a cheerful yellow, but a vague, unpleasant odor reminded her of the nursing home her grandmother died in. She shuddered.

They easily found the private room with Ellie Jenson's name beside the open door. Emily hoped she'd be willing to talk to them. When they peeked in, Emily saw right away that this was not a girlfriend or mistress. The white haired woman with wrinkly skin was sitting in bed, watching TV. She had to be in her seventies, if not older.

"Mrs. Jenson," said Henry. "May we come in? We're acquaintances of Carter Jenson."

"Carter? You knew Carter?" Her eyes got teary. "My poor baby died you know. Terrible thing. The police came to my door all dressed in their ironed uniforms, and I said to myself *Uh-oh. Why are they here? Are they coming for me?* Then they asked if I was Carter's mother, no, next of kin, that's how they put it. I said I was and then they told me the awful news."

"We're so sorry for your loss," said Emily. "Did your son visit often?"

"He came just about every month. Sent me chocolates, too. I love chocolates. He's all I had. Now I'm going to die here all alone."

"We're helping the police investigate his murder," lied Emily. "Have you been a patient here for long?"

"Decades. After the accident, Carter whisked me away from Boston, to overseas, then he put me here. I couldn't walk anymore. He was hoping they'd be able to fix me, but I've not been able to use my legs ever since." She looked across the room at her wheelchair, which was parked between the end of the bed and the bathroom.

"When did you see your son last?" said Emily.

"Not too long ago. He was real upset. I have a grandson, you know. Not that I've ever seen him in the flesh. Just pictures. He's three. Anyhow, Carter says to me that I don't have a grandchild any more. I says to him, 'What do you mean?' and he tells me his wife lied to him and he just found out he wasn't little Jimmy's father!"

"That's awful! What did his wife say about it?"

"She was going to take him, and Carter wouldn't ever see him again. He wasn't his father and had no right to custody or visits. Carter was mad. Fuming mad. Said he was going to take care of the problem."

"What did he mean by that?"

A nurse entered, carrying a dinner tray. "I'm sorry, but visiting hours are over. Mrs. Ellie needs to eat and keep up her strength, isn't that right, Mrs. Ellie?"

"Yeah, yeah. There better be chocolate cake on that tray for dessert. Or pudding. I like chocolate pudding, too."

Emily said, "Enjoy your dinner. It was very nice meeting you, and again, we're so sorry about your son."

They stepped out in the hall just as the elevator doors closed. "I know whoever was in there saw us. You'd think they could've held the door," said Emily. "I'm going to make darn sure we teach Maddy how important it is to have manners."

"I think Fiona gave her a good start. Hey, it's only two floors. It will be back soon."

"So what do you think about all that? Carter *did* know about Jimmy. He'd just found out recently and was hopping mad. If he threatened to take Jimmy, or hurt Holly—"

"Maybe Holly decided to strike first," said Henry.

Chapter 25

The next morning, Emily walked into her classroom, where Holly and Logan were waiting. Logan had his notebook open on the desk and Emily peeked over his shoulder, assuming he was working on his book. Instead, she saw sketches.

"Logan, I didn't know you were an artist," said Emily.

"This is hardly art. More of an invention. I've been inventing since I was a little kid. You know how kids are addicted to their smart phones these days, even in my fifth grade class. I've designed an app which is like a scavenger hunt, like geocaching, if you know what that is. It will get the kids up and out of their seats."

"Well, I hear all the time how kids sit around and play video games all day. Anything that gets them up and moving is a win."

"Sounds like *Pokemon Go*. It's already been done," said Holly.

Emily whispered in Holly's ear. "Come into the hall for a minute. I have something to ask you."

Holly followed her out. The others hadn't yet arrived.

"Last night, Henry and I took a ride to see Carter's mother."

"Carter's mother? She's been dead a long time. She died before I even met Carter, while he was in graduate school at Harvard."

"She's in a long term care facility about an hour from here."

"That's impossible."

"Her name is Ellie Jenson. Does that sound right? She knew all about Jimmy and even knew Carter wasn't his father."

"Why would Carter have lied about his mother being alive? It doesn't make a bit of sense."

"You'd know better than I would. Didn't you wonder about his out of town trips? He saw her almost every month."

"So that's where he was. He told me he was going on business trips, but I figured he had a girlfriend stashed away somewhere. After what I did with Wichita, I couldn't exactly be self-righteous, even if Carter didn't know about it."

Emily saw Tessa and Maria coming down the hall. "Let's go inside."

"Mrs. Fox, how did your mystery hunt go?" said Tessa.

"I'm afraid I'm more puzzled than ever." Tessa looked at Holly, who shook her head.

Maria said, "Holly, I'm glad to see you here."

"Dad insisted I take a break. He's at the hospital with Jimmy. I said I'd come here at least for part of the day."

"Is Jimmy doing better?"

"Yes, much. They're putting the casts on later and think he can go home in a day or two."

Just as Emily gathered her notes, Wichita, late as usual, scooted in next to Holly.

"Today we're going to work on plot. One of the hardest things to do as an author is to keep the plot moving. You don't want your book to sag in the middle, so think of an unexpected event to write into the middle of your works."

Tessa said, "You mean like a murder?"

"Or a case of mistaken identity," said Logan.

"Yes, those are both good examples. Your goal is to surprise the reader and make him want to keep reading to the end. Take some time and see what you come up with."

Emily circulated while they worked. The morning flew by, and before she knew it, it was time for lunch at Coralee's. The Outside Inn was by far the group favorite.

As usual, Coralee greeted them at the door. "Holly, Franklin says Jimmy might come home in a day or two."

"Yes, I can't wait. He's getting his casts today."

They sat at a round table near the window, overlooking the golf course. Coralee announced the specials, leaving menus on the table as well.

"I'm having that goat cheese quiche I had last week," said Tessa. "It melts in your mouth. Wichita, didn't you order that also?"

"Sure did. Didn't know I liked goat cheese, but it was delicious. I'm hoping she has lava cake for dessert. It's worth the indulgence." He slapped his own hand. "Better stop with the sweets or I'm going to wind up diabetic, like my cat!"

Emily, who was facing the window, heard stomping and swung her head around. Franklin approached the table and slammed a document down in front of Wichita.

"Sign this," said Franklin, "and maybe I won't kill you after all."

Wichita scanned through it. "I'm not signing this; are you crazy? You want me to relinquish all parental rights? I'm Jimmy's father. Now that Carter's dead, I'm the only father he'll know."

"I'm warning you," said Franklin.

Holly grabbed the paper from Wichita. "Dad, are you crazy? You can't ask him to do that."

"I sure can."

"Dad, let's get back over to the hospital. Jimmy will be looking for us."

Franklin grumbled, grabbed the document, and stormed out with Holly.

Tessa said, "That man has passion." She ran her tongue across her top lip.

"Nothing sexier than a little passion," said Maria. "Mmm Mmm."

The group continued eating their lunches. All except Wichita. Even after Franklin left, he seemed agitated, tapping his fingers and constantly scanning the room. His plate was the only one that hadn't been licked clean.

"Let's get back to work," said Emily. On the way out, she passed that weird stranger in the three-piece suit. *What does he want from Sugarbury Falls and how long is he going to stay?*

Chapter 26

Back at home after class, Emily decided to do some cleaning. With the vacuum running, she didn't hear Henry come through the door.

"Boy, you should have heard the fight at the hospital just now," said Henry.

"You startled me. Wait, let me turn this off. Now, what did you say?"

"I went to check on Jimmy before I left the hospital. As usual, Holly was in his room, and Wichita was there, too. Before I even opened the door, I heard yelling. Wichita was saying something about getting married and I heard Holly laugh. Then she told him *not in a million years.*

"Really? Poor Jimmy was right there and those two were fighting loud enough that you could hear them in the hallway?"

Henry took off his tie and unbuttoned his shirt. "That's the size of it. Anyway, Wichita said something about getting custody and that would mean he'd have access to Jimmy's trust fund. Then Holly said something to the effect of *over my dead body.* Then Wichita stormed out. I don't think he even noticed me, but Holly's face was red like she was embarrassed."

Emily said, "Maybe that was Wichita's plan all along. Think about it. With Carter dead, he could marry Holly and share in Jimmy's wealth. Oh, and I forgot. At lunch, Wichita mentioned having a diabetic cat. You know what that means, don't you?"

"He'd have to give the cat insulin shots…with a hypodermic needle."

"We know he had financial troubles, severe enough that he was going to lose his house. And Carter rejected his big idea—Dino-WOW-ica@—which he seemed to have been counting on."

"And one more key piece of information. Holly once said Carter often rode his bike home after work because the traffic was so bad. She said he had a drawer full of biking supplies in his desk. They were business associates. I'll bet Wichita was in and out of that office all the time. He'd of had plenty of opportunities to inject those gel pack with whatever killed Carter. It didn't matter if Carter died at work, at home, or here, in Vermont."

"Let's call Detective Wooster and tell him about the fight and the needles and Wichita being Jimmy's dad."

Emily was about to call the station when she heard sobbing coming from Maddy's bedroom. "Let me check on her."

Emily knocked on the partially open door, then walked in and saw Maddy stretched out on the bed, crying. One of the photo albums was open on the bed.

"Maddy, are you okay?" She sat on the bed next to her and put her hand on Maddy's back.

"I…miss…my…Mom." Maddy was crying so uncontrollably, Emily worried she wouldn't be able to catch her breath. She went to hug Maddy, who pulled away from her. "You're not my mom and you can't take her place."

Emily felt completely helpless. She ached, not from Maddy's words, but because she wished she could make things better. She sat silent on the bed, hoping her presence would mean something.

Henry called from the living room. "Should we start dinner?"

"I'll be right there." She stood up and said, "I miss her too. Your mom was smart and so much fun to be around. I'll never take her place, but Henry and I will help you in whatever way we can." She sat back down on the bed for a while longer before returning to the living room.

"How is she?" asked Henry.

"She's having a tough time—missing her mother."

"Poor thing. It's going to take time."

Emily turned her head toward the front door. "Who's knocking? We weren't expecting anyone."

"I'll get it. I called the detective while you were with Maddy."

"Good evening, Detective Wooster. Emily and I have information that may help move the investigation forward. Come, sit down."

"Let's hear it," said the detective.

"We recently found out that Wichita Johnson, not Carter Jenson, is the father of Holly's baby. Wichita knew about it, but Carter just recently found out," said Henry.

"Wichita wants to marry Holly and that would give him access to Jimmy's inheritance," said Emily. "Holly wants no part of getting married."

Emily and Henry went on to tell him about Wichita's access to hypodermic needles and to the gel energy packets. They also mentioned the odd packages, the white powder, and how Wichita was stealing money from the company to fund his project.

Emily said, "The clues are pointing toward Wichita Johnson. He had a strong motive for killing Carter. Marrying Holly would make his financial problems disappear."

"And he had the means to murder him—access to Carter's energy gels, and a supply of hypodermic needles."

"I appreciate you calling me," said Detective Wooster. "If you hear anything else, please get in touch."

Emily expected more of a reaction from Detective Wooster. Just like his partner, he kept his emotions under wraps.

"We will. Thanks, Detective." Henry showed him out.

Maddy, red-eyed with tear-damp hair clinging to her face, came out of her room and said, "Can I help make dinner? I can tear the lettuce for the salad."

Chapter 27

Emily had just pulled into the parking lot of St. Edwards the next morning when she received an urgent text from Coralee asking her to come immediately to the inn. She quickly scribbled a note saying she'd be late, and stuck it into the classroom door. Then she hopped back into her Audi and sped over to the inn. When she arrived, police cars were parked at the entrance and an ambulance screamed to a stop right in front of her.

Oh my God, this doesn't look good. Someone is hurt.

She ran to the entrance, but crime scene tape blocked the way. Guests, many wearing bathrobes and pajamas, huddled in groups across the lawn. Coralee, standing just outside of the tape said, "Emily, I'm so glad you're here." Her hands were trembling.

"What's going on, Coralee?"

"Oh, good heavens I wish I knew. I came down to the lobby at the crack of dawn like I always do and…"

"And what? What did you see? Had someone broken in?"

"No, it's worse. Much worse. He's…dead. There's been a murder."

Emily's heart fluttered. "A murder? Who?" She tried to peek inside the inn, but couldn't see much from where she was standing. She did notice blood spattered on the door.

She said to the EMT who'd just arrived, "What's going on?"

"Ma'am, step back and let us through." The EMTs wheeled a stretcher inside.

"Coralee, is it Noah? Tell me it isn't Noah!" She faced her, placing her hands on Coralee's shoulders and looking her straight in the eyes.

"No." Coralee exhaled. "Thank God it's not him."

Reporters carrying cameras tried to push their way inside but were stopped by officers guarding the entrance.

Pat jumped out of the coroner's van, nodded to Emily, then disappeared inside. Emily heard more sirens, and saw Detectives Wooster and O'Leary questioning guests on the front lawn. She saw flashes of light from the reporters' cameras.

"Coralee, who was murdered? Look at me."

"I…it's one of your students."

"Who? Which one?"

"The tall one with the funny name."

"Wichita? Wichita Johnson?"

"Yes, him. Wichita Johnson."

Emily's heart dropped. Wichita? Just when they'd convinced themselves Wichita was a murderer, it turns out he's a victim? It didn't make sense.

"Coralee, how did he die?"

"He was shot. I found him face down. Blood was coming out."

"Did you hear a gun shot?"

"No. The police said whoever did it must have used a silencer because it would certainly have been noticeable otherwise."

Emily heard Henry calling her name. He ran up and hugged her.

"Emily, are you okay? What's going on? I saw Pat fly out of the hospital, and all these police cars?"

Tessa, Maria, and Logan finished talking to Detective O'Leary and ran across the lawn to where Emily, Henry, and Coralee were standing.

"Mrs. Fox," said Maria, "Do you know what happened? They wouldn't let us into the lobby. They made all the guests come out the back door. Then they were asking us questions."

"I've read enough mystery novels to know that with this many cops, an ambulance, and a coroner's van, there has to have been a murder," said Tessa. She turned her head in every direction. "Holly was going to the hospital to pick up Jimmy this morning. Where's Wichita? He was staying here with us."

"I'm afraid…" Emily was pushed aside by the EMTs carrying out a stretcher. The entire body was covered with a white sheet.

Franklin ran up to them. "It's Wichita, isn't it? I knew he was trouble. His sins caught up with him, right?"

Emily thought his comments were extremely odd and inappropriate, but she held her tongue. "Yes, it's Wichita. He was shot in the lobby. Coralee found him this morning."

Emily heard him mutter, "son of a b…" under his breath. *I wonder where Franklin was when Wichita was murdered. And I wonder if he owns a gun.*

"Emily," said Henry. "Can I see you for a minute?" He led her by the elbow away from the others. "The police are occupied up here now and I doubt they've gotten to this yet. I wonder if the drugs are still in Wichita's room. I want the police to look, however, if nothing's there, we're going to seem foolish."

"Are you suggesting we have a look? Sneak in through the back window?"

"You read my mind. Come on."

The police were still interviewing guests and the back of the inn hadn't garnered any attention at the moment. Henry held Emily's hand, and they scooted around the porch to the window of Wichita's room. The shade was pulled down, obstructing their view. Emily gently tried the window.

"It's not locked! Let's go in." She went in first, pulled up the shade, and raised the window as much as it would open. "Come on, the coast is clear."

Henry followed her inside. The bed was unmade and a pair of jeans and a t-shirt were draped over the desk chair. A half-full suitcase was open on the floor. Henry checked the closet and drawers. "His clothes are still here. Doesn't look like he was going anywhere."

Emily checked the bathroom. "His toothbrush and razor are here. I agree—he wasn't planning on leaving. What I don't see are the boxes of DVD's with bags of drugs underneath the Styrofoam noodles."

Henry rummaged through the suitcase and looked under the bed. Then he checked the shelf above the closet. "I don't see anything. He may have shipped everything off. There's no proof he ever had drugs in this room."

Emily got down on her hands and knees and rechecked under the bed. Then she pulled open the nightstand drawer. "Look, there aren't drugs but here's the box-cutter we saw him using the other day."

"Don't touch it," said Henry. "It's unlikely, I know, but there may be traces of drugs on it." His eyes fell on the open suitcase. "Emily, see if there's an outside pocket on his suitcase."

"Emily closed the top. "Yes, there is." She unzipped the pocket and stuck her hand inside. "Look, Henry. Little plastic bags. What do you suppose he was using these for? Dividing up the bigger bags of white powder, like we saw him doing the other day?"

Henry and Emily froze. Emily whispered, "Someone's right outside the door."

"Two people, at least. I heard a man's voice and a woman's. Let's get out of here."

They ran back to the window, pulling down the shade as it was when they entered. Emily swung her leg over the window sill and hopped out onto the porch, followed by Henry, who closed the window behind him. Making sure the coast was clear, they worked their way around to the front of the porch.

"I don't think anyone noticed us coming or going, do you?" said Emily.

Henry scanned the crowd. "No, but I think they're letting the guests back inside. Let's get out of here."

Chapter 28

Emily canceled the writing workshop for the rest of the day. It was barely lunch time, yet she felt like it was midnight. When they got home, Maddy, Chester nestled in her arms, came out of her room.

"I was watching TV and the news was on all morning. Someone was murdered at that place we had dinner at. Did you hear about it? Is that why you came home early?"

Emily answered, "Yes. It was one of my workshop students who was killed."

"What happened? Who got killed? I hope it wasn't Jimmy's mother."

"No, Maddy. It was a man named Wichita Johnson. He worked with Jimmy's mother, and her husband. Holly's husband, Carter, was supposed to be at the workshop also, but I found him lying at the bottom of a ravine one morning during my morning run—before you came here. It looked like a bike accident, but the police think it was murder."

Maddy's eyes widened, and with more animation than either Emily or Henry had yet seen from her, she said, "Two murders? In this little town? I grew up in Chicago and never once knew anyone personally who was murdered—or anyone who knew anyone who was murdered."

Henry said, "Don't get the wrong idea. It's not like murder is a daily occurrence around here. Chances are the two murders are related."

"Related? How? Did the same person kill them both? Is there a serial killer on the loose?"

"Calm down, Maddy. There's no serial killer."

"But the two men both worked together, right? Holly worked there too. Do you think she's next?"

Not only do we have to help Maddy cope with her mother's death and adjusting to a new town, now we have to assuage her fears about a serial killer running on the loose. Who knew parenting would be this complicated? Her stomach rumbled.

"Maddy, I have an idea. Since Henry and I are home today, why don't we pack a picnic and have lunch over by the lake?"

Henry jumped in. "That's a great idea. We have some ham and...I mean, we have cheese in the fridge. Let's make some sandwiches. Emily, don't you have some brownies in the freezer?"

"Sure do. I'll start making lunches. Henry, go change your clothes."

They hopped into the Jeep and drove to a picnic area by the lake. Shade trees and a wooden pavilion made the sun more bearable. Emily unpacked the cooler onto a wooden picnic table.

Maddy pointed. "What's that over there?"

"It's a covered bridge. Isn't it charming? There are still quite a few in this area. I'll bet you didn't see many of those in Chicago?"

She looked up at Henry, "Nope. You're right about that."

Emily poured lemonade into plastic cups, and Henry doused his hands with hand sanitizer, then tore open a bag of potato chips. While they were eating, Holly, wheeling Jimmy in a sturdy stroller, stopped at their table.

"Holly, good to see you out with Jimmy. Is he feeling okay?" asked Emily.

"I just brought him home from the hospital this morning. The casts are annoying him. I thought a little fresh air would do us both good. I also needed to get him away from the house, anyway. The police are there questioning my father. I can't believe Wichita is dead." She wiped her eyes with her sleeve.

Franklin had made that comment about Wichita deserving to be killed, and he has a prison record. Do the police suspect him?

Holly continued. "They're badgering my father about his gun. Yes, my dad owns a gun and it's all legal and registered. They asked to see it, but Dad said he didn't have it. He has a buddy who likes to go up into the mountains and hunt. He lent it to him."

"You mean like a shot gun?" said Henry.

"No, he has one of those too, and so does his friend. Dad lent him his revolver, for protection. His friend goes up into the woods by himself and feels better sleeping with a gun under his pillow in his little pup tent."

"Can't the police check out his story?"

"There's no phone service up there, and Dad has no idea where to find his friend. It's a big mountain. It'd take weeks to search it all."

"Surely your Dad knows when his friend is coming back," said Emily.

"No, he doesn't. It depends on the hunting and how the fish are biting. His friend is sometimes gone no more than a day or two, but he's been known to stay up there for weeks at a time. Of course, the police don't believe a word Dad is saying. Especially since some of the inn guests told the police they'd heard Dad and Wichita arguing. Someone even overheard him making a threat."

"I hate to say it," said Emily, "but your father didn't seem at all upset to find out Wichita was dead."

"Dad has always been overprotective of me, and was angry to find out Wichita was Jimmy's father. That doesn't make him a killer, though."

Jimmy fussed. "Mommy, I'm hungry."

Maddy picked up a brownie and broke it in half. "Can I give him this?"

"Sure, thanks," said Holly. "I'm going to take him home and give him lunch. Afterwards, maybe he'll get in a good nap. Poor kid has been through a lot." She wheeled Jimmy back down the path.

"A nap sounds like a good idea to me," said Emily. After they finished eating, they piled back into the Jeep and went back home. Maddy picked up the cat, then went into her room to read. Emily and Henry both lay down on the bed and were soon fast asleep. When they woke up, it was nearly dinner time.

"Flip on the TV," said Emily. "The local news should be starting. I'm sure the main story will be Wichita's murder. I'll go see what I can whip up for dinner."

Emily opened the fridge and found a spaghetti squash in the vegetable drawer. She also found a hunk of fresh mozzarella in there that needed to be used. Next, she opened the freezer. *Ground soy crumbles. I forgot I bought those.* Becoming guardian to a teenage vegetarian presented its challenges, not the least of which was cooking acceptable and tasty meals. She grabbed a mason jar of spaghetti sauce from the pantry.

Emily picked up the spaghetti squash and stared at it for a moment. *What if I microwave this sucker until it's soft enough to cut, then scoop out the seeds and scrape the strands of flesh into a bowl. I can mix together the strands of squash, crumbles, and sauce, then top it with the mozzarella and bake it. It will be like a vegetable baked ziti.*

Before the microwave had a chance to ding, Henry called to her from the living room. "Hey, it's on. They're showing the inn."

Emily wiped her hands on her apron and ran in. Henry and Maddy were seated on the sofa. The reporter said that a man had been found shot to death this morning at the Outside Inn and the police had just arrested Franklin Matherson.

"Oh, my God, they arrested Franklin! So soon? We just saw Holly a few hours ago."

"Em, I guess they didn't buy the story about his buddy borrowing his revolver, taking it to an unknown location somewhere in the mountains, and returning when the fish stop biting."

"Poor Holly. I can't imagine Franklin as a killer."

"The best thing that can happen is he gets that gun back. Then the police can prove whether or not it's the same gun that was used to shoot Wichita. It must be the same caliber. If the police didn't think there was good cause to suspect Franklin's gun was the murder weapon, they wouldn't have arrested him."

"I hope Franklin's buddy gets back soon. Poor Franklin. This will be tough on his heart condition."

"Emily, I hate to say it, but I hope there really is a friend who really borrowed that gun. You have to admit it sounds made up."

"Truth can be stranger than fiction, you know that. Franklin wouldn't risk going back to prison and leaving Holly and Jimmy to fend for themselves…would he?"

Chapter 29

I wonder what the mood will be this morning. Tessa, Maria, and Logan were all at the inn yesterday morning. They stood outside for hours, being questioned by the police, then waiting to get back inside. I already know how Holly must be feeling. I'll try to make the day interesting so they don't feel like coming here was more hassle than it was worth.

"Mrs. Fox, did you hear how they arrested poor Franklin?" said Tessa. She was wearing a cotton printed skirt, a white peasant top, and yet a different pair of designer eyeglasses—the third Emily had counted so far this summer.

"Tessa and I were just talking about how lonely Franklin must be, sitting in a jail cell, waiting for his friend to get back with his gun. We both know that sweet hunk of a man could never have killed anyone," said Maria. She applied coral lipstick form a Dior tube as she spoke.

"Maria and I were discussing baking him a cake."

"Yes, a cake with a file in it. Like in the old movies!"

Logan said, "Ladies, your focus is in entirely the wrong place. Wichita is dead. Wichita—our classmate. He's the one we should be concerned about."

Maria said, "Yes, poor Wichita. Only, he's dead and there's not much we can do for him now."

"Now Holly will have to run the company all by herself. And with her father in jail…poor Franklin, like a bird in a cage waiting to be freed."

Emily announced the topic for the day. "Let's talk about bringing our stories closure. The reader has been on a ride with us since he or she started reading. We don't want the ride to go on so long that it gets boring, nor do we want it to jerk to an abrupt finish. How do you plan to end your stories? Tessa?"

"Mine will end with the couple finally reaching Los Angeles and the husband succumbing to the arsenic poisoning. His wife will have him cremated and throw his ashes into the Pacific, freeing both her husband and herself."

Maria spoke next. "My teen heroine will lead her troops to triumph and become the leader of the new society. She'll free the handsome prince from jail and in the end, they will get married."

Tessa shook her head.

Emily said, "Both you and Tessa will end your stories in a way the reader will be left satisfied. How about yours, Logan?"

Logan, wearing jean shorts and a tan pullover, said, "The man whose idea was stolen will win in the end. He takes back his idea, makes a fortune, and everyone is happy that the tyrant boss is dead."

"You have a loose end," said Emily. "Who killed him? Your readers will want to know."

"I'm going to leave it hanging. Maybe I'll have to write a sequel."

Emily's phone vibrated. "Henry, I'm teaching let me step into the hall. Now, tell me. Okay, Franklin didn't have an alibi for the night Wichita was shot. Being home asleep sounds plausible to me. Didn't Holly verify it? Oh, that's right. She spent the night at the hospital with Jimmy. Did Pat do the autopsy? Let me guess, he died of a bullet wound. No kidding. And no sign of heart problems, or prescriptions for Digoxin? Okay, see you at home."

*****

After Henry hung up, he got into the Jeep. Instead of going home, he stopped by the inn to talk to Coralee. Something had been nagging at him ever since Wichita had been murdered. The inn was quiet when he arrived, and it smelled like Clorox. No one was out on the porch or on the golf course. Coralee was scrubbing the lobby floor.

"Hey, Coralee. Why are you scrubbing? Emily said a cleaning crew was going to take care of that as soon as the police were done with the crime scene."

"They were here, and I know I'm imagining it, but every time I look at the floor I see a puddle of blood. I can't get the image out of my mind. I have nightmares where I see Wichita bleeding and falling to the ground." She shuddered

"I can only imagine," said Henry. "Once the police catch the killer you'll be able to cope better. Emily doesn't think Franklin did it."

"Of course he didn't. I've worked with that man for a decade already. He's kind and helpful. I've seen a temper, but nothing that convinces me he'd pull out a gun and shoot someone in the head. You should see how great he is around Jimmy."

"Did the police go through Wichita's room?"

"They did. I'm the one who unlocked the door. Don't tell anyone, but I stood out in the hall and you know, kind of eavesdropped."

"Did they find anything?"

"No. I heard them say it was a dead end and they left. Didn't stay long at all."

"Remember all those packages Wichita got? Did he mail them back out?"

"As a matter of fact, only one or two. He brought them to the front desk and asked me to be sure the mailman saw them."

"He must have received half a dozen that I saw. I wonder where the rest of them are. Did the police carry boxes out?"

"No, they didn't. I hadn't thought about it, but you're right. Those boxes were heavy. I don't think he was getting boxes of cookies and eating the evidence or anything."

"What happened to that weird-looking guest who was here? You know, the one with the suit and the beard."

"He checked out the afternoon before Wichita was killed. Paid cash up front when he registered."

Wichita has boxes of DVDs with baggies of cocaine packed in them. He takes out some of the powder, then seals the boxes back up. Coralee says only two boxes were mailed back out, but Emily and I checked his room and there weren't any DVDs or cocaine. The police didn't find anything in there either. Meanwhile, a stranger shows up in town. Wichita sees him in the dining room and runs the other way. The man checks out of the inn the night before the murder. He prepaid in cash, and leaves no credit card behind by which to track him down.

While Henry was standing in the middle of the lobby, thinking, two men walked up to the desk and pulled out badges.

"Good afternoon, are you the owner?"

"I'm Coralee Saunders and, yes, I'm the owner. How can I help you?"

"Ma'am, we have a few questions for you. We're with the FBI."

Chapter 30

Emily made a pan of baked ziti and a spinach salad for dinner. She was expanding her repertoire of vegetarian dishes and, so far, Maddy had eaten everything she'd made. She called Henry and Maddy to the table. Henry came in, took a deep breath, and announced that it smelled delicious.

"How was your day, Maddy?" said Emily.

"Okay. I went on line to look up Sugarbury High. The entire high school has fewer students than what I had in my eighth grade class back in Chicago. The demographics are pretty different too."

Demographics? And I noticed she's been finishing the Sudoku puzzles Henry starts and abandons. This girl is one smart cookie, just like Fiona was.

"It's small, but from what I hear, it's a good school. The marching band was in the Memorial Day Parade. One of my co-workers has a daughter who goes there. Maybe I can introduce you. She works on the yearbook. What kind of things are you interested in?" said Emily. She caught herself acting overly enthusiastic once again.

"I like animals. I told my Mom I wanted to be a veterinarian when I grew up. Every year for my birthday and Christmas she got me something to do with that. Last Christmas she got me a real stethoscope. For my birthday, she got me a subscription to *Canine Cornucopia.*" Maddy paused, her eyes narrowing. "What's going to happen to my magazines? They're going to be sent to our old apartment."

"We filled out a change of address form. It may take longer at first, but you'll get them."

Henry said, "I'm sure we have a 4-H club in town. I can look into it."

"You mean raising farm animals? The kind they bring to state fairs and weigh and give out ribbons? No thanks."

They ate in an awkward silence for a few minutes. Maddy wiped a tear with her napkin.

"Emily, I went by Coralee's after work and guess who came in? The FBI."

"Selling drugs across state lines is a federal offense. Maybe they were on to Wichita. Too bad all the evidence was gone. All except for the box cutter and baggies. I hope the police found those items when they searched."

Maddy looked up. "Drugs? That guy who was shot, was he shot for dealing drugs?"

Emily wondered if they should be talking about this in front of Maddy. "We don't really know. It's possible."

They had almost finished eating when they heard a knock on the door.

"I'll get it." Henry invited Kurt inside.

"I got Prancer with me. I don't know if you want him inside. He's a good boy, but his paws may be a little dirty."

"Come in, both of you," said Emily. "There's plenty of ziti left. Let me get you a plate."

Kurt didn't object. He sat down at the table next to Maddy, Prancer beside him. Chester crept into the dining room, spotted Prancer, and high tailed it into Maddy's room. Maddy pet the top of Prancer's head, and the chocolate lab started licking her. Emily hadn't seen her smile so brightly since she'd been with them.

"That dog likes you," said Kurt. "He's a good judge of character, he doesn't like just anybody."

"Want a beer?" said Henry.

"Sure, if you've got one. I came over to tell you what I heard this afternoon. I was downtown picking up some supplies at the hardware store, then I got hungry, so I went next door to the pizza joint. I'm sittin' there, and these two suits come in and sit at the table next to me. We were the only ones in the place—it was too late for lunch and too early for dinner."

Henry set the beer on the table. "So what'd you hear?"

"The two men, I'm positive they were FBI. They're talking about a murdered guy and my ears perked up. I pretended I was busy on my phone, but if I was a dog like Prancer here, you'd have seen my ears standing straight up at attention."

Emily leaned in. "Maybe we shouldn't talk about this now," She darted her eyes toward Maddy.

"What, you're worried about talking in front of the kid? Don't let her fool you. When Chloe was her age there was practically nothing she didn't know about."

Maddy smiled at him and he continued. "They was sayin' how the victim, that's how they referred to him, was transporting cocaine through the mail. They'd been watching him for a while. When Carter got murdered and they knew Wichita was in town, they got suspicious."

"Do they think Wichita kill Carter because he knew about the drugs?" said Emily.

"No, they talked about that. That's what I wanted to tell you. They said when Carter, well, they said 'his boss,' was murdered, they had Wichita on tape doing a deal. In fact, he was so busy receiving packages, siphoning cocaine out for himself to sell, then resending the rest along with the work packages that he couldn't have done it. They'd have known."

Maddy, still petting the dog, said, "It's obvious why he was murdered. Sounds like he was skimming off the merchandise, taking some of the drugs out and selling them privately. The dealers he was working for caught on and bam. They knocked him off. You don't screw around with drug dealers." Her Chicago street smarts emerged out of nowhere.

"That's why he had his own supply of baggies," said Emily. Did they arrest the dealer?"

Kurt said, "I don't know. They stopped talking. I think maybe they wondered if I was listening." He finished the last of his ziti. Maddy had gone to the floor and Prancer was on his back, enjoying belly rubs. "Hey, Maddy, that's your name, right? You should come over and play with Prancer sometime, or even take him for a walk if you want and it's okay with your parents."

Parents? Is it okay to be called her parents? If not, what should they be referred to as? Guardians sounded stilted, and once she was at school, she'd feel odd calling us by our first names... Maddy hadn't flinched. She was preoccupied petting Prancer.

"Of course. She's welcome to visit or walk Prancer whenever she wants."

After Kurt left, Coralee called to talk to Emily. Henry listened at her side and got the full scoop after they hung up.

"Well? What was that all about?" said Henry.

"Coralee says the FBI men came back and asked her more questions. Do you think the bearded man in the suit was FBI?"

Henry rubbed his chin. "Could be why Wichita was avoiding him. Maybe he's the one who took the remaining boxes out of Wichita's room—for evidence. Did they make an arrest?"

"Not as far as Coralee knows. She didn't have much information to give them. If they do arrest him, at least Franklin will be off the hook."

"And we know Wichita didn't kill Carter." Henry looked at Maddy and Emily." So who did?"

Chapter 31

That night, Emily wondered about whether or not Holly would continue with the workshop. Franklin was in jail, and Jimmy couldn't attend Tiny Tots in his condition. As if she'd read her mind, Holly called after dinner, asking if Maddy could babysit Jimmy the next day. She told Emily she wouldn't be helping Franklin by sitting at home, and she wanted to keep her mind occupied. Maddy smiled when Emily asked her about it, and spent the rest of the night looking on-line for arts and crafts ideas.

The next morning, Holly arrived early at class. "Good morning, Mrs. Fox," said Holly. She wore a printed sundress and her hair was piled in a loose bun. "Jimmy took to Maddy right away. I'm sure he'll be happy. Before I left, Maddy had already found the watercolors and was painting with him. He loves to paint."

"It will be good for Maddy, too. So far she has spent every day sitting in the cabin while Henry and I are at work. I couldn't interest her in swimming lessons or dance class."

"Did you hear? Wichita didn't kill Carter. He had an alibi. He was shipping cocaine hidden in boxes of DVDs the company was sending out. The police told me he was stealing some of those drugs and selling them on the side, like double dipping. I heard the FBI had had their eye on him for some time. They'd have seen him planning or committing Carter's murder if he had. It's hard to believe. You think you know someone."

Tessa and Maria walked in. Tessa hugged Holly and said, "Holly, dear. How's your father doing?"

"He's not happy sitting in prison for something he didn't do. The police act like they don't believe him when he says his friend has his gun. If the friend would just show up, they could test the gun and prove the bullet that killed Wichita didn't come from it."

Maria said, "Are they allowing visitors? I could go by and cheer him up."

Logan walked in and unpacked his notebook from his backpack. He was wearing basketball shorts and a sweaty t-shirt, and carrying a bike helmet.

Emily said, "Logan, did you ride your bike from the inn?"

"Yeah. Had to. I've gained five pounds already this summer eating Coralee's cooking. My cardiologist is threatening to up my meds."

"I have a writing exercise for us to start with. I want you to pick a time when you experienced an overwhelming emotion. Maybe the day you got married or at a friend's funeral, then write a paragraph or two showing that emotion."

Emily circulated while they worked. She thought about Maddy and how she was easing herself into the community by babysitting and making friends with Kurt. So far, things were going okay. She enjoyed watching TV with Maddy and shopping together. What she didn't enjoy was trying to read Maddy's mood. If she asked her a question, she never knew whether she'd get a cheerful answer, or be snapped at. When it looked like everyone was done writing, she resumed class.

"Since there are only four of you, why don't you each read your passage aloud, and the class will give you feedback. We will try to guess what emotion you are portraying. You're all good writers, so it shouldn't be too difficult."

As usual, Tessa volunteered to start things off.

The call was one a mother should never, ever have to receive. The voice on the end of the line told me to hurry to Boston General; my son was involved in an accident. They refused to give me information over the phone. I was too shaken to drive, so my neighbor volunteered to take me to him. When I got there and saw him, my heart cracked like an eggshell. He was gone, without explanation and at the hand of a drunk driver. I yelled, punched the wall, fell to my knees. I don't remember how I got back home.

"Grief," said Maria. "The yelling, punching, her being shaken—I felt her pain."

"Good," said Emily. "I think your example was very clear."

"I'll go," said Logan.

My entire body trembled when I saw him. I felt the heat rise to the top of my head. We'd been friends once. We'd lost touch, as friends sometimes do, but I had no idea how he'd betrayed me. Not until that moment, in the middle of a crowd, face to face after so many years.

Holly said, "It's obviously anger he's showing. His old friend did something horrible to him, but he didn't realize it until the moment he saw him, after many years."

Maria read next.

Yes, I was older than most. The interns could have been my grandchildren. We were told to make a presentation. I colored a poster, stood up, and talked about my idea. The others had slide shows, power points, sound effects...I knew each of them inside was laughing at this old lady past her prime, an antique.

"I'd say embarrassment or worthlessness. Been there, done that," said Logan.

Holly read a paragraph about the day Jimmy was born, showing joy, pride, and love.

They went their separate ways for lunch. Emily had arranged to meet Henry in the hospital cafeteria. She spent a few minutes organizing her notes for the afternoon. When she got to the parking lot, she saw a black car speeding away. It was as if the car had been parked, waiting for her to come out, then changed its mind. She couldn't be certain, after all, there were tons of black cars on the road, but was it possible? Was that the same black car that had followed them to Sweet Water Manor?

Emily pulled into the hospital parking lot and texted Henry that she was on her way to the cafeteria. Once inside, the clanging pots and banging trays made her slight headache worsen. She spotted Henry at a table, waved, and proceeded through the line, picking out the healthiest options she could find—minestrone soup, a turkey sandwich, and an apple. Then she had a vision of a turkey in a tiny wire cage, and swapped the sandwich for a veggie wrap.

"So how was your morning with the 'wanna-be'...I mean, how was the morning with your writers?"

"It went well. I'm glad Holly came. Hear anything about Franklin or the FBI?"

"Pat said there were no traces of drugs in Wichita's body—no cocaine or Digoxin, so I did a little hunting and looked up Franklin's heart pills."

"Let me guess. Digoxin?"

"No, it wasn't. It was an entirely different drug Digoxin is for heart arrhythmias. Franklin's on a beta blocker. Speaking of which, Franklin isn't very compliant about taking his meds. Holly picked up his last prescription, but before that, he hadn't refilled it for months."

"Is that important?"

"When Franklin came into the emergency room, I noticed he had a bad tremor in his right hand. I saw it again at Coralee's. In order to fill a syringe with liquid Digoxin and inject it in a tiny hole into the gel pack, you can't have shaky hands. Now, a beta blocker can calm down a tremor, but he wasn't taking it! I don't think he could have pulled off poisoning the gel. Besides, he owns a gun, and has been in prison for assault with a deadly weapon. If he wanted to kill Carter, I don't think he would have considered such a subtle and unpredictable method as a drug overdose."

"I think you're right. He didn't have access to Digoxin, had a hand tremor, and owned a gun. So now where are we? We know Wichita didn't kill Carter because he was being followed by the FBI, and Franklin lacked the means to do it."

Henry said, "Of our original suspects, we are left with Holly."

"But did she have access to the drug? We know she lied about seeing Carter and that she was worried he'd try to get full custody of Jimmy. That's a strong motive."

Emily took a bite of her apple. The lunch rush was in full swing and the noise, paired with her headache, made it difficult to concentrate.

Henry said, "If only we could find some sort of proof linking Holly to Carter's murder. If it isn't her, who else? Did anyone else in your writing group know him beforehand?"

"I don't think so, I assume they would have mentioned it. Carter, Wichita, and Tessa all live or at one time lived in Boston. Logan and Carter went to school together in North Carolina. Maria isn't even from the east coast. She flew in from San Diego."

"Flew in from San Diego? I'm sure they have plenty of summer writing workshops in California. How much do you know about her?"

Emily was so flattered when Maria said she loved her book on the Ashley Young case and had to be in her workshop, that she didn't question it. "I guess I don't know much at all."

"I think it's time to start digging."

Chapter 32

When Emily got home after the workshop, she heard Henry and Maddy's voices coming from the kitchen. "Hi, guys. I'm home. What smells so good?" She walked in and saw Maddy tearing lettuce and cutting tomatoes, while Henry diced tofu into a frying pan with bean sprouts, broccoli, and ginger. She loved the smell of fresh ginger.

Henry gave her a kiss. "How was the rest of the day?"

"It went well. I tried to nudge Maria about her reason for coming to my workshop, but she stuck with her original story." She puffed out her chest and cleared her throat. "She wanted to work with the *New York Times* Best Selling author—you know, the one who wrote the infamous true crime book on the Ashley Young case."

"Okay, okay. So maybe that's all it was."

Maddy said, "You're a *New York Times* Best Selling author? I knew you wrote books but I had no idea you were famous."

Is she impressed, or is she being sarcastic?

"It was one book and I was only on the list for twelve weeks." She gathered dishes and forks. "I'm working on another, though." As she set the dining room table, she said, "How was babysitting?"

"I think I had as much fun as Jimmy. We painted, played Candyland, made animals out of Play-doh, and ate Oreos."

"I'm sure both Jimmy and Holly really appreciated it."

"Holly seems like a good mom. She's really caring. Even her neighbor said so."

"Her neighbor?"

"Yeah, an old lady who lives next door. She brought over some roses for Holly. She said Holly helps her with lots of things, like shopping and doing errands. She said Holly even helped give her insulin injections when she was first diagnosed with Type 2 Diabetes. I can't imagine giving yourself a shot."

Shots, needles, did her neighbor take Digoxin?

After dinner, Emily and Henry sat down with her laptop. Henry had gotten good at finding public databases after all the reading he'd been doing about private investigating.

"Em, what's Maria's last name?"

"Mendez. Really unique, right? I'm sure there are thousands of women with that name."

"You just have to know how to filter. She lives in San Diego and is in—what—her early sixties?"

"I think so."

"You said she writes teen fiction and she's a librarian. Probably belongs to a librarian's association, or maybe an educators' group." He clicked some keys. "I'll bet she's joined some writing groups as well—Mystery Writers of America…Sisters in Crime…"

Maddy said, "What are you doing?"

Henry, feeling his face flush, answered, "Doing a little investigating. We're trying to help the police find Carter Jenson's killer. He's the dead biker Emily found." He explained how he was going about his search. Maddy stared over his shoulder, absorbing everything.

After a while, he announced, "Aha! Got it. She did live in Boston. She worked at a public library. Even got an award, "Children's Librarian of the Year" for the state of Massachusetts."

"What year?" said Emily.

"2000. When was Carter at Harvard?"

Emily searched. "He graduated with his Masters from Harvard in 2001. So they both lived in Boston at the same time. She never mentioned it."

Maddy said, "Boston's a big city. Just because they lived there at the same time, doesn't mean they knew each other. It's like when someone says they live in China, and then someone tells them their old neighbor lives in China. Like they're bound to know each other or something."

"Maddy's right. We have to find out if she actually knew Carter. Can you ask her?"

"I suppose, but if she's guilty, why would she admit to knowing him? Besides, we haven't a hint of a motive. I'll see what I can do when I see her tomorrow."

Maddy said, "You need to dig deeper." She took the computer from Henry and googled. She sifted through various articles. "Here's the newspaper article about when she got the librarian award. The easiest thing would be for you to friend her on Facebook, Emily. You can get a lot of information there."

Emily went to her account and sent out a friend request, hoping Maria was on social media. "Meanwhile, let's look up Carter Jenson."

Maddy still had the computer on her lap. She verified the spelling, then googled him.

"He's got pages of entries. Successful businessman...inventor of Matha-WOW-ica@...says he premiered the new Story-WOW-ica@ prototype last spring at the National Educator's Conference in Rochester, N.Y."

"Rochester? One of the participants lives in Rochester. And he's in the education field. I wonder if they met there. Hey, come to think of it, they both lived in North Carolina, too. Look up where he went to college."

Maddy scrolled and clicked, then said, "He graduated from The University of North Carolina at Chapel Hill."

"Write down the date for me," said Emily. "Now, can you google Logan Park. He's a fifth grade teacher in Rochester."

Maddy went back to work. "He's harder to find. There's a Logan Park, attorney, Logan Park's Plumbing Co., Logan Park, accountant...Did you know there's a town in California called Logan Park?"

Henry said, "Look him up under UNC alumni or Department of Education—both in North Carolina and New York."

Maddy stayed focused, clicking and scrolling while Henry and Emily waited. "Snap. I got it." She scribbled down the graduation date. "He graduated the same year as Carter Jenson. Let's see what else we have...Hey, he was at that conference in Rochester last spring also. He presented a workshop."

"That's a pretty uncanny coincidence, don't you think? He never let on that he knew Carter," said Emily.

"Remember what Maddy said. Just because you live in China doesn't mean you know everyone else who lives there too. Logan is a teacher and he lives in Rochester. Of course, he'd go when the national convention showed up on his doorstep. And Carter went to present his idea. It could be coincidental. They may have crossed paths there but never met."

"And they both graduated from the same university, the same year?"

"Chapel Hill has at least 20,000 students. Again, could just be coincidental. You'll have to ask Logan directly."

Emily picked up her phone. "Maria accepted my friend request."

Maddy said, "When you have time, scroll through her profile, and see who her friends are."

Emily's phone vibrated on the coffee table. "It's my brother, Robbie."

"Hey, Robbie, how are the girls? We're doing fine. Tell me. Really? Three times? And he had a DUI? This private investigator knows what he's doing. Yes, keep him on. I'll send you money through PayPal, it's quicker than mailing it. Great. I can't wait for you to meet Maddy. She's very smart. I think she likes it here. Thanksgiving for sure. Talk to you later."

"News about your mother?" said Henry.

"Robbie hired a private investigator like I told you, and get this. Mom's new fiancé has been married three times. All of them died under questionable circumstances. And he has a DUI on his record. Robbie cares more than I do. If Mom is that stupid about who she chooses to go out with, that's her problem, not mine."

They exchanged the laptops for a 1000 piece jigsaw puzzle. Maddy had mentioned she liked doing puzzles, so Henry had ordered one on Amazon.

Opening the brand new box, he said "I think we should start with the corners."

With everyone's contribution, the puzzle was well under way by bedtime.

Chapter 33

The next morning, Emily dropped Maddy off at Holly's to watch Jimmy. When she walked Maddy inside, she smelled strong coffee—perfume to her taste buds. Remnants of breakfast, bits of scrambled eggs, stray Cheerios and a yellow sippy-cup, formed a random design on the table in front of Jimmy's booster seat.

"Mrs. Fox, thanks for dropping her off. Getting Jimmy in and out of the car seat with his casts on isn't easy. He's really looking forward to seeing Maddy again. That's all he talked about last night."

"I had fun, too," said Maddy. "Where is he?"

"In his room. Go on up."

Emily waited until she stopped hearing Maddy's feet on the steps. "Babysitting has been good for Maddy. She loves Jimmy, and she's pretty impressed with you, too."

"Impressed? Why?"

"She thinks you're a great mother and a super nice person. After all, Jimmy is so bright for his age, and apparently a neighbor stopped by and told her what a help you were. Something about giving her insulin injections."

"She must mean Sally. Gave her insulin shots? That was many years ago when I visited here one summer. Jimmy wasn't even born yet. I'm surprised she remembered that."

"Kind deeds don't go unnoticed. Have you heard anything more about your father's friend?"

"Not yet. Can I get you some coffee?" She pulled down a mug before waiting for the answer.

"I'd love some. You know, it occurred to me that Logan is from Rochester, and that big educational conference was there last spring. Wichita had said he and Carter went there to roll out Story-WOW-ica@. Did you go with them?"

"No, I stayed home with Jimmy and kept an eye on things at work. Why?"

"I'll bet Logan was there. Funny, he probably crossed paths with Carter and never knew it."

"Carter crossed paths with tons of people at that convention. Some friendly and enthusiastic, others nasty naysayers. One night he called and sounded very shaken up. It was unlike Carter. Almost nothing bothered him. He didn't go into details, just said he'd had an unpleasant encounter and something about a jealous competitor. Anyhow, next time we talked, he sounded like his old self, so I guess it was no big deal in the end."

Emily looked at her watch. "I've got to get moving. See you in a few minutes."

Holly's the only one with a strong motive to have killed Carter. But why didn't Logan mention being at the convention with Carter and knowing about Story-WOW-ica@? And Maria never mentioned having lived in Boston. I'm probably grasping at straws, but I hate to think of Holly as a murderer.

Emily hoped to question Maria about Boston and Logan about the Educator's Convention. She saw Maria on the way in from the parking lot.

"Good morning, Maria. I love your necklace. Did you get it at the craft fair?"

"I did. I love artsy jewelry. By the way, I accepted your friend request on Facebook. Now we can stay in touch after the workshop is over."

"That's what I was thinking. I'll do the same with the others since we live so spread out. Speaking of living spread out, did you always live in San Diego?"

"I grew up there, but I spent a few years working in Boston. Had a wonderful job, and a not so hot relationship. When we broke up, I moved back home. I try to forget I ever lived there with him."

"You know, Tessa is from Boston, and Carter went to graduate school at Harvard. Did you ever run into either of them while you lived there?"

Maria laughed. "No, Boston's a big city. That's like meeting someone from Nebraska and saying 'My aunt lives there. Do you know her?' I wished I'd have met Tessa while I was there. I'm sure we would have been friends. Had I been lucky, she'd have stolen that jerk of a boyfriend away from me and saved me lots of grief! As far as Carter Jenson? Never even heard of the guy until I came here."

Emily believed her. Now she'd try to corner Logan. Once inside, they all got right to work, revising what they'd written the previous day. Emily made her way over to Logan.

"Logan, I was wondering if you'd ever met Carter. He was dead before you got here, and you might not have a face to put with a name. I noticed that the two of you both did your undergraduate degrees at UNC-Chapel Hill at the same time."

"UNC is a big school. You basically only know the people in the same department or dorm."

"Then I was thinking, Carter presented his prototype for Story-WOW-ica@ at the National Educator's Convention last spring in Rochester. You live in Rochester. I thought it would be funny if the two of you had actually known each other and you just didn't recognize his name."

"I don't know the name, and I don't even remember going by a Story-WOW-ica@ display. I gave a presentation at the convention. I was pretty nervous, and I didn't spend a lot of time wandering through the displays."

Tessa called her over. "Which verb tense should I use here? Past or past perfect? It always confuses me."

While Emily was helping Tessa, she saw her phone vibrating on her desk. She normally would have ignored it, but since Maddy was watching Jimmy all by herself, she wanted to be available. "Got it, Tessa? I'll be right back."

She wandered over to the desk and saw a voicemail from Maddy. She listened to an urgent message and called her back.

"Maddy, what's wrong?"

"He's…someone's outside the house. He knocked and I peeked through the curtain. He... looks so scary. He has a beard and…and a lumberjack shirt. His hair and face are filthy. I ignored the knock."

"Is he gone?"

"No! That's why I called you. I took Jimmy upstairs with me to his bedroom and waited for him to go away. He kept knocking, then went around to the back and knocked. Then he yelled, *Open up. I know you're in there.* I'm so scared."

"I'll be right there. I'll call the police on the way."

"Wait. Here's the worst thing. I looked out the bedroom window and I saw something bulging out of his pocket. Emily, he has a gun!"

Chapter 34

Emily grabbed her phone and her purse. "I'm sorry. I... have to go. It's an emergency. Holly, come with me."

"Is it Jimmy? Did something happen to him? You're scaring me."

"Jimmy is fine. Come on." Emily grabbed her by the elbow and dragged her out of the classroom.

She barely gave Holly time to shut the car door before she sped off in her Audi. Holly was shaking and begging for details.

"Holly, call 911. Tell them there's a prowler outside your house."

"What! A prowler? But..."

"Just hurry and call." The cars in front of her slowed down.

Come on, what's the hold up? She pressed her horn over and over again, but the traffic wasn't moving. "Holly, can you see anything?"

She opened the passenger side window and stuck her head out. "I think a car is stuck on the railroad tracks." With the window open, the cacophony of honking horns in itself sounded like a freight train approaching. "Wait, the police are coming; I hear sirens."

Emily drummed her fingers on the steering wheel. *If anything happens to Maddy or Jimmy, I'll never be able to forgive myself. Fourteen? What was I thinking letting her babysit?* She honked the horn. "Can you see anything else? Are they getting the car out of the way?"

"I can't tell."

They sat for what seemed like hours. Emily called Henry and told him to meet them at Holly's. Finally, the car in front of her inched up. "I think we're moving now."

Holly said, "I see a tow truck ahead. We're going now."

"Thank God." She pressed her foot all the way to the floor. "We're almost there." Her heart pounded like a jackhammer. *I hope we get there in time. What if we're too late?*

They finally pulled into the driveway, behind a police cruiser. She and Holly flew into the house where they saw a police officer, a man in handcuffs, and Maddy clutching a crying Jimmy. Holly ran to them and grabbed Jimmy, smothering him with kisses. Emily grabbed Maddy close.

"We've got him," said the officer. "And we have the gun."

A second officer entered. "No one else is outside. Looks like he was working alone."

"Wait," said the lumberjack look-alike. "I can explain. My name's Edmund. I'm Franklin's friend."

"You know my dad?" said Holly. She turned to Emily. "I never met his friend face to face."

"Yeah. He lent me his gun for my hunting trip. I just came to return it to him. I saw someone moving upstairs, so I figured he didn't hear me or something. He's a little hard of hearing sometimes."

The police officer said, "You're coming downtown. You and the gun. I understand your buddy's locked up in a cell. We'll have to get an ID from him."

Emily said, "That's the gun! Franklin told the police he had a gun but he lent it to his friend for a hunting trip. Holly, maybe this will get your father out of jail."

The officer said, "Even if this guy's story checks out, we'll have to send the gun to ballistics and see if it's the one that killed the victim."

Henry ran into the house and absorbed the scene. A scrubby man in handcuffs, the police holding a gun." What's going on here? Are you okay?"

Emily, still clutching Maddy, inched her way over. "Yes, we're all okay. Our girl did the right thing. She heard a prowler but didn't answer the door, which she had made certain was locked, and she called me."

Henry kissed Maddy on the top of her head. "I'm proud of you, Maddy. And glad everyone is unharmed. Let me take you both home. You can tell me all about it in the car."

All three were silent for the rest of the ride.

As soon as they got home, Emily flopped down on the sofa and kicked off her shoes. The scare had made her realize how deeply protective she already felt about Maddy. When she'd decided not to have children, it wasn't because she was averse to the responsibility it entailed. She'd been confident she and Henry could provide for a child, both financially and emotionally. Not inclined toward globe hopping, they weren't worried about being tied down.

It was the vulnerability. She'd seen what had happened to her mother after her sister had died, how it had changed her as a person, how a part of her had died, and the remainder became an impulsive, needy mess. And Tessa. When she talked about her son being hit by that car, her eyes reflected so much pain after so many years. She couldn't yet use the word *love*, but every day she felt closer to Maddy. Like she was a part of their lives. Was she starting to care too much?

"How about we work on our jigsaw puzzle?" said Henry. Maddy shrugged her shoulders.

Emily said, "Great idea. Something to keep our minds off of this morning."

They spent the afternoon working together on the puzzle. Henry, impressed with Maddy's concentration and perseverance, said "You've got an aptitude for problem solving. Did you get that from your Mom?" He saw Maddy's eyes tear up and wished he could take the words back.

"Yeah. When I was little, Mom and I put together those painted wooden puzzles. When I got a little older we did jigsaw puzzles, but not like this. They had fewer and larger pieces."

They worked for a few more minutes before Maddy said, "I'm going to take a nap."

"Good idea," said Emily. "I think I'll do the same. How about we go to the inn for dinner?"

"Whatever." She grabbed Chester from the sofa and slammed the door of her room.

"Henry said, "I was so stupid, bringing up her mother. Now she's upset."

"Maddy is going to have memories about her mom. We don't want to pretend Fiona never existed. I read in *Teenage Parenting for Dummies* how their emotions can swing on a dime. Don't worry, you didn't do anything wrong."

"I guess it's unrealistic to think she won't have times when she misses her mother."

"You know it is. Come on. Want to join me for a nap?"

Chapter 35

Emily's eyes bolted open. She had set the alarm on her phone so they wouldn't nap so long that it would interfere with a good night's sleep later on. She nudged Henry.

"I'm up. Should we get ready for dinner?" Henry rolled out of his side of the bed and pulled on his jeans.

Emily washed off her face and changed into navy blue Bermuda shorts and a turquoise, J. Crew polo shirt. "Let's see if Maddy's awake."

Henry followed her down the ladder, and they both knocked on Maddy's door.

"Maddy, can we come in? We're going to dinner. Are you up?"

Henry said, "Knock again. She's probably still asleep."

After another round of knocking, waiting, and no response, Emily gently opened the door. "Where is she? The bed's empty. Check the kitchen." She heard noises coming from the guest bathroom. *Thank God. She must be in there.*

Emily yelled to Henry, "I'll check the bathroom." The bathroom door was ajar. When she glanced inside, her heart fell to her knees. The noise she'd heard was just Chester using the litterbox.

Henry checked the kitchen and dining room. "She's not here, but the back door is unlocked." *We always lock that door, but Maddy doesn't have a key.*

Emily told herself not to panic, but her first thought was that the man claiming to be Franklin's buddy, had been released from the police station and had kidnapped Maddy. Maddy was the one who'd got him caught. Maybe he wanted revenge. She expressed her concerns to Henry.

"I think you're overreacting. Maybe she just needed some air. Let's see if she's outside."

They went out the back door, calling Maddy's name. "Let's try down by the lake," said Henry.

"She doesn't know how to swim. What if she was so upset about her mother, she didn't pay attention and fell in?"

"Emily, what's with you today? You've been reading too many mystery novels. Come on."

They ran down to Lake Pleasant, but there was no sign of her.

"Let's go back and check the barn." He knew it was also locked, but Maddy was petite enough, maybe she'd squeezed in somehow. He ran to the front of the barn. The lock was still intact. Then he pulled open the side door. "Maddy, are you here?" A month ago she could have easily hidden, but he'd recently purged the place to set up a woodworking studio. "I don't see her."

"Should we call the police?"

"Not yet. Let's check the other direction. I still think she most likely went for a walk."

They followed the road to Kurt's house. Henry pounded on the door. Kurt noticed everything that went on in the neighborhood. Maybe he'd seen her. The door flew open.

"Hey, come in. I was just about to walk this little lady back home." Maddy was sitting on Kurt's living room rug, playing with Prancer.

"Maddy! You scared us half to death," said Emily. "We didn't know where you were. I thought...never mind."

"I'm sorry. You and Henry were upstairs taking a nap. I didn't want to wake you. I just took a little walk, then ran into Kurt and Prancer. It was so hot outside, he said I could come in and play with Prancer for a little while. I didn't mean to scare you."

Henry took a deep breath and let the adrenaline subside. "Next time, leave a note. We were worried something had happened to you. Are you ready to go eat?"

She shrugged her shoulders. "I guess so."

Emily said, "Kurt, why don't you come with us to Coralee's for dinner. Unless you have other plans."

"That sounds good. I was about to pop a Hungry Man dinner into the microwave, but the food at Coralee's will definitely be tastier." He gathered his things and jumped in the Jeep.

When they got to the inn, there was a small line waiting to be seated. The Maddy drama had brought them to dinner later than usual, during the evening rush.

Tessa came downstairs and fell into line behind them. "Mrs. Fox, I'm so glad everything turned out okay earlier. I called Holly and she told me what had happened."

"Everything worked out okay." She saw no use in relaying the missing Maddy story. "Are you eating alone?"

"Yes. Maria has a headache and didn't want to come downstairs. Logan mentioned something about ordering pizza." Her eyes fell on Kurt. "Who's your handsome friend?" She batted her eyelashes at Kurt.

"Tessa Carlisle, this is Kurt Olav. He's our next door neighbor." Emily couldn't believe it, but Tessa was already eyeing Kurt. "Would you like to join us?"

"I'd love to," Tessa said. "If it isn't an imposition."

Kurt said, "Not at all. Dinner with three lovely ladies, who'd object to that?" He lightly nudged Henry in the ribs with his elbow. Maddy rolled her eyes at Emily.

Coralee scooted around, mingling with the guests. The hostess seated them at a round table in the center of the dining room.

Maddy crinkled her nose. "I smell fish. It smells gross."

Emily silently agreed with her, while reminding Maddy of the newly added vegetarian options.

As soon as they'd ordered, Tessa began giving Kurt the third degree. "So where are you from, Kurt? Is there a wife in the picture, or children?"

"I'm from Minnesota. It'll always be in my blood, but when I got divorced, I wanted to get as far away from my ex-wife as possible. I have a grown daughter, Chloe."

"Tessa is from Boston," said Emily. "She's one of my summer writing students. Very talented."

"Don't make me blush," said Tessa. She turned her attention back to Kurt. "Does your daughter live here?"

"No, and I'm not comfortable discussing her. How about you? You got any kids?"

Tessa squirmed in her seat. "I had a son, but he was run over by a drunk driver. Right as we were about to go to trial, the old lady disappeared off the face of the earth. She must have had help disappearing, being paralyzed in the accident and all."

"You never found her?" asked Maddy, joining the conversation. "She got away with murder? That's so not fair."

"No. I didn't find her back then. I had a private investigator working on it for years. Turned up nothing, thought it was a waste of money."

Kurt said, "Have you found her now?"

"Not yet, but I'm real close. A few months ago I caught a break all on my own. I was watching *60*

Minutes, like I do most Sundays, and they were interviewing a rich inventor/businessman. I recognized the last name from back when the accident happened. He said on the show he was spending the summer in Vermont, so I did some digging."

So that's why she's really here. I'd like to think my workshop was the reason, but Tessa has been looking for this woman for years. She chooses my workshop, and coincidentally, she's recently received information that this lady is here in Vermont.

"What'd you find out?" asked Kurt.

"This rich son of hers had to be hiding and supporting her. Get real, how's a paralyzed old lady going to hold down a job? But there's been a recent development."

Tessa can sure tell a story. All of us are glued to her words. Writing's a good hobby for her. Maybe she'll sell that book she's working on.

Maddy said, "What development?"

"I found out her son died recently. She's on her own now. Before that old lady kicks the bucket, she's going to pay for what she did."

Chapter 36

"Henry, are you about ready?" said Emily.

The story Tessa had told last night about the drunk driver who'd killed her son and then disappeared, stuck a chord with her. As soon as they left dinner, she asked Henry if he thought she was crazy to think Carter's mother was the one Tessa was after. Henry had been wondering the same thing. It was Saturday, and they were both free to take another ride to Sweet Water Manor. Emily left pancake batter in the fridge and a note on the table for Maddy, in case she happened to wake up before lunch time.

"I'll drive," said Emily. She loved the feel of her new Audi and looked forward to flying over the country roads on a traffic light Saturday morning.

"Be my guest." Henry closed his eyes in the passenger seat, eventually drifting into sleep.

Emily coasted along the road. When they were just about at their destination, she spotted a small black car keeping its distance behind her. *I'll bet that's the same car as last time. Who's following us and what interest do they have in Sweet Water Manor?* She said Henry's name, but realizing he was asleep, didn't disturb him. She kept checking the rear view mirror. For a while, she thought the car was gone, but thought she caught a glimpse of it as she pulled into the parking lot of the facility.

"Henry, we're here. Wake up."

"Here already? Man, I never fall asleep in cars but your Audi rides so smoothly it practically rocks you to sleep. You're welcome." Henry had bought the car for Emily as a surprise, after her old car had wound up in Lake Pleasant.

They receptionist remembered them from the last visit and waved them on. When they got to Ellie Carter's room, she was sitting up in bed, eating pale scrambled eggs.

"Hello, Mrs. Carter. We're back again."

"Seeing as I don't get a whole lot of visitors—make that none now that Carter's gone—you're welcome to visit anytime. You can call me Ellie, you know."

Henry pulled two chairs up to the side of the bed. "We have a few questions for you. What happened that got you into this place? Were you always paralyzed?"

"Heavens, no. It's hard to talk about. I accidently ran over a pedestrian and killed him. The car swerved, hit a shade tree next to the sidewalk, and I flipped over. I was in a coma for a while. When I woke up, I was paralyzed."

"Did you go to jail for killing the pedestrian?"

"It was an accident. The boy's mother pressed charges, thought I did it on purpose or something. Carter said he didn't want me to end up in jail. I needed to recover, not to be in a prison cell, especially since I didn't do anything wrong."

Emily said, "So what happened next?"

"Carter did a bunch of research. Found a surgeon in a clinic over in Switzerland who had performed miracles on people who were never supposed to walk again. Carter said he could help me, so we went there."

"I'm guessing he wasn't able to help you," said Henry.

"He tried. I went through half a dozen surgeries, stayed in a rehab clinic for a long time, hoping the surgery would eventually prove successful, but it didn't. When it became clear that I wasn't going to recover the use of my legs, Carter whisked me back to the states and found this place."

"Why didn't you go live with him?" asked Emily. *And why did your son tell his wife you were dead.*

"Carter was afraid that kid's mother, after all these years, was still after me. He wanted me safely out of sight. I know I did nothing wrong, but Carter said good lawyers put plenty of innocent people in jail. I was scared, so I agreed to stay here."

"Here's my number," said Emily. "If you ever need anything, call us. We're not too far from here."

"Thank you. Enjoy your day now. I'm getting a manicure this morning after breakfast. They have a lady who comes here on Saturdays."

"I'm sure you'll enjoy it. Bye now." Emily took Henry's hand and led him into the hallway.

"The mother of the kid she ran over—it has to be Tessa," said Emily.

"Sounds like it, only Ellie skipped over the part about drunken driving. Guess if I was Carter, I'd have done the same thing. I wouldn't have let my mom go to prison either."

"Not sure I can say the same, but that's beside the point. Let's get back home. Tessa has motive. She must have been planning this for a long time. We have to tell the detectives."

Emily again got behind the wheel. She'd barely gotten to the main road, when she spotted the black car again. "Henry, that black car behind us, it was tailing me on the way here. And I think it's the same one I saw the first time we came up here."

Henry looked out his side window. "I see it, but why would it be following us?"

Emily sped up. The black car followed suit. Then she deliberately slowed down, allowing it to pass her, but instead, it slowed down as well. *I'm getting to the bottom of this once and for all.* She whipped her car around, transversing the road. The black car had no option but to stop. Emily and Henry ran out of the car and up to the driver's side door. Emily yanked the door open.

"Tessa! Why were you following us?"

Tessa stumbled out of the car. "I knew it. I knew the woman who killed my son was Carter Jenson's mother. After all these years, I found her. I can't wait to call the police."

"Just calm down, Tessa. She claims it was an accident."

"Yeah, I heard. I was listening outside the door when she told you that pathetic story. She conveniently left out the most important detail. She was drunk when it happened."

Henry moved the Audi out of the middle of the road. "Let's have a seat in Emily's car."

Emily said, "She's an old lady now, but you're right. She took your son's life. The thing is, aren't you even now?"

"What are you talking about?"

"I know you found out Carter was coming to the workshop from *60 Minutes.* You followed him here and poisoned his energy gel with Digoxin."

"You're crazy. I'm no killer. And what's Digoxin?"

"If you go to the police and explain…"

"Explain what? I wasn't even in the country. I flew into Vermont straight from London, where I'd spent the past month. You can check it yourself. I probably still have the boarding pass in my suitcase back at the inn."

Emily believed her. "Let's go back to town. You can tell the police she's here and they'll probably arrest her right away."

Tessa shook her head. Tears streamed down her face. "I can't. All these years it's all I thought about, but after seeing that frail old lady, I'm not sure sending her to jail is the right thing to do. Do you think I'm crazy?"

"Not at all. You have to do what you feel is best. Sometimes that's forgiveness."

"I'm thinking I'll let it go. She lost her son, even if it wasn't at my hand. She'll die there all alone. That's sentence enough."

Chapter 37

When Henry and Emily got back home, Maddy was sitting at the coffee table, working on the jigsaw puzzle. "How did it go?"

Emily said, "I feel a renewed faith in humanity. My student, Tessa, gave up a well justified vendetta against her son's killer."

"That's good, I guess. Want to help?"

"Sure. Henry, come help us too."

Maddy had completed the entire edge of the puzzle while they'd been were gone. Emily fit a few pieces together, completing one of the corners. Emily's phone vibrated.

"Hi, Holly. Everything okay? What? Really? That's terrific news. I'm sure you and Jimmy couldn't be happier. Thanks for telling me."

"Well?" said Henry.

"Ballistics came back. The gun did belong to Franklin, but it wasn't the one used to kill Wichita. Franklin's story about lending it to his buddy turned out to be true after all. I'm happy for them."

"It still leaves the question of who killed Wichita. And who killed Carter. It's not Tessa. It wasn't Franklin since he has that hand tremor and doesn't have access to Digoxin, and it wasn't Wichita, who was under surveillance for drug dealing. Maria, although she briefly lived in Boston at the same time as Carter, had no reason to kill him that we know of."

"The only two with a connection to Carter we haven't ruled out are Holly and Logan." Emily connected the section of puzzle she was working on to the corner section.

"Holly wouldn't kill anyone," said Maddy. "She's a mother. Mothers aren't evil killers."

This time it was Emily who rolled her eyes. Naïve Maddy had no idea how creepy some mothers could be. Her phone vibrated again.

Speak of the devil. "Hey, Robbie. What's up?" Really? Then that's good news, right? She's going to visit you while she sorts things out? Better you than me. Seriously, I'm sorry, Robbie. Keep me posted."

"Your brother?" said Henry.

"Yes. The private investigator said Mom's fiancé vanished. Cleaned out my mother's jewelry box first. Anyway, Robbie got a call from Mom. She's super upset and is going there for a visit."

Maddy fit two more pieces together. "Who's Logan? What makes him a suspect?"

"He's in my writing class. I have no idea why he would have killed Carter, I only know that he didn't admit to knowing him, yet they were both at UNC at the same time, and they crossed paths again at an educational convention in Rochester last spring."

Maddy said, "Think of the usual reasons someone hurts someone. Were they in love with the same woman? Was he being blackmailed by Carter? Did it involve money?"

Emily thought about it. "Holly showed no signs of ever having met Logan when she saw him in class. She married Carter after he was finished with school, and I remember that Holly made a comment about never having been to North Carolina during one of our classes."

"What about blackmail? If they went to college together, maybe Logan stole the answers to a test or raped a sorority girl at a party."

"Maddy!" said Henry. "Raped a girl at a party? That's one of the first things you thought of when you thought college?"

Emily said, "The media plays that sort of rare event up, but Maddy, that's not the norm."

"Okay, okay. So he stole the school mascot. Or snuck beer into the dorm."

"She may be onto something," said Henry.

"There's also revenge. Like you said about Tessa having a vendetta," said Maddy. "I hear thunder. Is it supposed to rain?"

Emily peeked out the window. "Sky is getting pretty dark. Maybe you should run over to the store and pick up something to make for dinner. I found a spinach lasagna recipe, but I don't have spinach or ricotta cheese."

"Okay. Maddy, do you want to take a ride with me?"

"Sure. But only if we get some ice cream for dessert. Look, we only have a few more pieces left before we finish."

Emily ran the vacuum and straightened up the guest bathroom. She'd have to talk to Maddy about not throwing the wet towels on the floor, and not getting toothpaste all over the sink. She thought she heard a knock on the door, but the thunder had gotten louder so she wasn't sure. There. It was a knock.

"Logan, what are you doing here? How did you know where I lived?"

"Coralee told me. I have to tell you something. It's about Holly. Something I heard her saying to her father."

"What is it?"

"I wanted to run it by you before going to the police. It might be nothing."

"Logan, just tell me."

"Okay. She was talking to Franklin at the inn after he came home from jail. She said something like, 'Hope I never wind up in there for what I did. He deserved it, though'."

"Do you think she meant she killed Carter?"

"Yeah. She also said it was worth the effort, poking through those gel packs and breaking a few needles. She thanked Franklin for letting her use his heart medicine to do the job."

The thunder was right overhead. Chester meowed and darted under the kitchen table.

Franklin's heart medicine. Pat said the poison in the gel packs was definitely Digoxin, but Henry confirmed that that wasn't the medication Franklin was on. Besides, how did Logan even know about the gel packs and the needle? The police were keeping that information quiet. Her legs trembled.

"Logan, let's call the police right now."

"I'd rather go over in person. Sounds like a downpour. Mind if I wait here till it lets up?"

"Of course not. Have a seat. Would you like some coffee?"

Logan nodded his head. Then he looked down at the coffee table. "Some puzzle you got here. Looks complicated, but you've almost finished it."

"It's been a group effort." She felt in her short's pocket. Thank goodness she'd put the phone in there while she was cleaning. Normally she left it out on the coffee table. She went into the kitchen, then pulled out the phone and tried Henry. *Why isn't he answering?* Next, she scrolled through her contacts for Detective Wooster's number. Maybe she could keep Logan here until he came to arrest him. She was about to punch in the number, when…

"Give me the phone." Logan held out his palm. "Now."

Emily was shaking from head to toe. She handed him the phone, never having heard Logan use that tone of voice before.

"Logan, let me finish making the coffee and we'll talk. We'll talk about how Holly killed Carter."

Logan laughed. "Don't try and play me. I could tell by the expression on your face you didn't believe me. Then you snuck off to make a call." He looked at the phone. "Detective Ronald Wooster. Well what do you know?"

"Logan, why did you kill Carter. I mean, if you killed Carter."

"Oh, I killed him alright. Fate stepped in last spring at the educator's convention. Back in college we were best buddies. He majored in business, I double majored in education and computer programming. We lived in the same dorm freshman year, then shared an apartment the rest of the time we were there. I had this great idea for an educational game. Matha-WOW-ica@. Started as a class assignment. I told Carter all about it. He didn't think it'd work. At least that's what he said."

"So you invented Matha-WOW-ica@, not Carter."

"That's right. Carter was a business major and told me all the reasons it wouldn't work. Market share, restricted consumer base—blah, blah, blah. I went ahead anyway and applied for a patent. It was denied. The patent office said they had a similar patent pending. Shrugged my shoulders and gave up."

"Did Carter steal the idea?"

"Never crossed my mind, but he sure did. He manufactured the program and went on to become a millionaire and form his own company. I wound up teaching fifth grade. In truth, I'd seen Matha-WOW-ica@ in educational catalogs, but it never crossed my mind it was my idea from back in college. Then I went to that convention."

"And you saw Carter there."

"I saw him behind a display table. I don't think he even knew who I was at first. He was showing off his new product—Story-WOW-ica@. He had it set up for people to try, so I tried it and guess what? It all came together. I gave Matha-WOW-ica@ a try, too. He was showing that also. It was my game, down to the minutest detail. I felt my blood boiling under my collar."

"What did you say to him?"

"Nothing. I was too dumbfounded to speak. He invited me to drop by his room later that night for a drink. Spoke about old times. I decided then and there to plan my revenge. He talked about biking. We used to ride together in college on the weekends. He showed me his fancy bike and had a box of energy gels sitting on the nightstand. Couldn't believe he'd taken his bike to Rochester with him, but he was hard core about it. Said he'd read about some great trails up in the mountains."

Hurry up, Henry. Where are you? It shouldn't be taking so long.

"Tell me what happened next."

"He told me all about the summer writing workshop and how he wanted to attend so he could tweak his new product. Then he invited me to come too, since I was a teacher and he figured I taught writing. He even had this idea about meeting a few days early and doing some biking. He'd read there were great riding paths in Vermont."

Emily inched toward the front door, praying Henry would get home. "So you took him up on it. How did you get the Digoxin and the needles?"

"I told you I had heart issues. Stomach issues too. That's why my cardiologist gave me an injectable form of—drum roll, please—Digoxin. It was almost too easy.

I met him in his hotel room, injected the gel pack while he was in the bathroom, and told him I'd meet him in the morning for a ride. That morning, I told him I felt sick and he should go alone. And the rest …well, you know the rest."

"Henry will be home any minute now. You should get out of here before he does. Run far away— somewhere the police won't find you."

"And leave you behind to tell my little tale? No way." He grabbed her hands and pulled them behind her back. She struggled every which way, surprised at how strong he was. He pulled her toward the door. She ducked down and away, breaking his grip. He stood between her and the door, so she ran the other way. *Think, Emily. Henry will be home soon. I just have to stall him.*

She darted into the guest bathroom and locked the door. Logan started pounding on it. "Get out, it's useless." He pulled the handle.

She felt sweat soaking through her shirt. He started pounding with something heavy. The fireplace poker! She knew if he kept at it, the flimsy wooden door would eventually break. She looked around the bathroom and grabbed the can of Scrubbing Bubbles she'd been using to clean. She took a deep breath. *Here goes. Now or never.* She put her finger on the button and flung open the bathroom door. As soon as she saw his face, she held her finger on the button and sprayed half the can into his eyes. Then she ran for it, while Logan, blinded, screamed in pain. She pulled open the front door, and fell into Henry's arms. The police were right behind him.

Henry kissed her and held her tight. "Are you okay?"

"I am now. Where's Maddy?"

"I made her wait in the car. You can thank her for getting the police here. She noticed you had tried my phone and tried to call you back, but you didn't answer. She said she knew something was wrong, so I called the police and got home as soon as I could. The rain slowed us down."

The police slapped handcuffs on Logan, still complaining about his burning eyes. When they drove away, Henry got Maddy from the car. Maddy ran to Emily and hugged her tight. It was the first time she'd ever hugged Emily, and whether it was the let down or adrenaline, or the realization that Maddy cared about her, tears streamed down her face. They clung to each other for a long time.

Chapter 38

Emily went to bed early and woke up late the next morning. What a summer! Finally, Carter's killer was behind bars. Logan had killed Carter because he stole his idea. Just like in the book he was writing. She wished she'd paid closer attention. One loose end remained. Who killed Wichita?

"Hey, I smell coffee," said Emily. In the kitchen, Maddy was dipping pieces of raisin bread into a mixture of eggs and cinnamon, while Henry flipped French toast slices in the frying pan.

"There's local maple syrup on the table," said Maddy, smiling at Emily.

"What a nice treat. Detective Wooster asked me to go by the police station this morning to sign a statement. After that, I'm holding a final writing session to make up for the time I missed. Tessa and Maria are flying home tomorrow morning. I'm going to miss them."

"There's always next summer," said Henry.

Emily didn't want to think that far ahead. After today, she wanted to relax and spend time with her family before school started up again. She looked forward to doing something she'd never done before—back-to-school shopping.

To celebrate the end of the writing workshop, and solving Carter's murder, they were all getting together for a farewell dinner at Coralee's that night.

"This is the best French toast, ever," said Emily. "You two will have to do the cooking more often." She finish every last bite, then helped straighten up the kitchen before going to the station.

Detective Wooster was waiting for her in his office. "Thanks for coming down. Hope you had a good night's sleep. You deserved it."

"I'm glad this is all behind us. Only one thing is still bothering me. Who killed Wichita Johnson? Did you figure it out?"

"We got the guy. Mr. Johnson was involved with some shady characters. The drug dealer he was working with figured out that fewer drugs were arriving at their destination than what he'd shipped out. He found out Mr. Johnson was skimming cocaine out of the packages before sending them, and selling what he stole on the side, keeping a nice profit for himself. The dealer followed him here and shot him point blank."

"By any chance, was it a bearded guy who stayed at the inn?"

"Sure was. He'll be behind bars until that beard is completely gray. Here, if you could sign the statement you gave us last night."

Emily signed the statement. On her way out, Detective O'Leary came in wearing designer jeans and a cute peasant top. It was the first time Emily had seen her wearing makeup.

She looked over her shoulder and saw Detective Wooster step out of his office and give her a peck on the cheek. Then he asked her if she was ready to go to lunch. *Now those two make a cute couple. Romance is blooming in Sugarbury Falls. Better romance, than murder!*

She met Holly, Tessa, and Maria in the classroom. "Looks like we're finishing with half the people we started with," said Emily.

"But it's the better half," said Tessa. "Hey, I finished my book last night. Can't wait for you to read it."

"That's terrific. I'm looking forward to reading it," said Emily. "So I assume the husband dies and the wife lives happily ever after in Las Vegas."

"Oh, no. I changed the ending. The wife finds forgiveness in her heart, and starts feeding her husband the arsenic antidote. He recovers and they renew their marriage vows. Then they live happily ever after together—in Vegas."

"When we forgive, it frees us. Great theme you've got, Tessa," said Holly. "In my book, the single mother takes over her dead husband's company, making billions of dollars thanks to the changes she institutes. Her little boy grows up and becomes CEO."

"Freeing the mother to retire and run off to Bora Bora with a handsome surgeon," said Tessa. "I like that."

"How does your story end, Maria?" said Emily.

"You know my female protagonist has to rise to the top. She leads an army to overcome the resistance and her peers elect her president of the new nation. She builds a library on every corner. Same old story."

"Are you going to write another true crime book, Mrs. Fox? You certainly have some new material," said Tessa.

"I will," said Emily. "But first I think I'll write some contemporary fiction. There's this couple who never thought they wanted children, but they wind up being guardians to a teenage girl. The rest is, as they say, unwritten."

"Well, I'm sure hoping for a happy ending," said Tessa.

Holly walked out with Emily. "Mrs. Fox, I want to ask you something."

"Sure, Holly. What is it?"

"You have the address of the place Carter's mother is staying in, right?"

"I do."

"I've been giving it a lot of thought, and I'd like to go and meet her. I want to bring Jimmy, too. I'll be living here, not too far from her. I was married to her son, and she has no one now."

"Holly, that's a wonderful idea. I'll text you the address."

On her way home, Emily felt a wave of gratitude wash over her. She truly loved living in Sugarbury Falls, she had a great start on her new crime book, and she felt like Maddy was becoming part of their family. When she walked in the front door, Maddy and Henry were working on the puzzle. Maddy snapped in the last piece.

"There. Puzzle is complete," said Maddy.

On the table was a picture of a path through the woods, dark at the bottom of the puzzle, gradually becoming lighter, topped off with a rainbow.

THE END

ABOUT THE AUTHOR

 Diane Weiner is a veteran public school teacher and mother of four children. She has enjoyed reading for as long as she can remember. She has fond memories of reading Nancy Drew and Mary Higgins Clark on snowy weekend afternoons in upstate New York and yearned to write books that would bring that kind of enjoyment to her readers. Being an animal lover, she is a vegetarian and shares her home with two adorable cats and a little white dog. In her free time, she enjoys running, attending community theater productions, and spending time with her family (especially going to the mall with her teenage daughter and getting Dairy Queen afterwards).

A Deadly Course is the first book in her Sugarbury Falls Mystery series. She also writes the Susan Wiles Schoolhouse mysteries.

www.ingramcontent.com/pod-product-compliance
Lightning Source LLC
Chambersburg PA
CBHW020332260626
47156CB00004B/1493